MY FENCE IS ELECTRIC

AND OTHER STORIES

MARK NEWMAN

ODYSSEY
BOOKS

Published by Odyssey Books in 2020
www.odysseybooks.com.au

A catalogue record for this book is available from the National Library of Australia

ISBN: 978-1922311030 (paperback)
ISBN: 978-1922311047 (ebook)

Cover design by Michelle Lovi

For Mike

BEFORE THERE WERE HOUSES, THIS WAS ALL FIELDS

WHEN I WAS at the end of my childhood, Susie Banshawe disappeared. For a while no one knew where she was, and that was the best of it. There was a sense of excitement, each of us hoping we would be the first to discover a clue, without really understanding what that meant.

We lived on a street called Crunching Croft and I bussed into school at Maple Bumpstead. It was like something out of a fairy tale, so we should have known. Give a housing estate a fairy tale name and something evil is bound to follow. But what would we have done with a happily ever after? To live happily ever after, to be happy day in, day out, and never to be plagued by nightmares when you slept. It would be as exhausting as being permanently unhappy. We are not meant to be one thing at all times.

It was a new estate, still being developed, new buildings popping up all the time. We had a house you could run a circuit round inside. Is that unusual? I have not lived in a house like it since. From the hallway to the living room to the dining room to the kitchen and back into the hallway. You always had forward momentum. Even in the lounge if I wanted to get to the hall I would run through the dining room, into the kitchen and out into the hall again. I had my own one-way system in force.

All the houses were the same: little clones appearing. Across from us, an almighty pit had been dug, and around it more houses were being built. We ran around investigating, my best friend Jammy and I, standing at the edge of the pit and looking down. It was the first place anyone thought of looking of course; they'd had teams down there, winching sniffer dogs down in pulleys, but with nothing to show for it. The shells of those half-built houses stood around, all bricks, breeze blocks, and concrete. They were like skulls, no windows in the eye sockets, and ladders propped where the stairs would be. Jammy and I clambered up those ladders and launched ourselves from upstairs windows onto mounds of sand below. There was no Health and Safety in those days; or if there was, nobody took much notice. When those houses were finished I stood in front of them, full of all the impressive knowledge you can feel when you're ten: I have seen your skull, I have seen you without your skin. I thought I knew those houses better than the people who lived in them. In some way they were all interlopers, spoiling my fun.

We had the run of the place, us kids. The best thing we did was follow the dustbin men. They let us sling the smaller things into the back of the truck. I loved the clang of the metal teeth, the way they devoured it all, whatever you fed them. I loved the smell of all that rotten food and the guys with their fluorescent clothes, their hands and faces covered in muck. They were feeling important too; the police had asked them to watch for anything being chucked that could give them a lead.

'You should come back to my place sometime,' one of them said. 'The things I find that people throw out, you wouldn't believe.'

'He's starting his own junk shop,' another one said. 'It's all there in his front room.'

They laughed a lot and slapped each other on the shoulders.

When they did the same to Jammy and I, we thought we were real men, grown up and ready to face the world.

Policemen were appearing at odd moments all over the place; we got used to seeing them about. I ran into one down an alleyway. He asked if I'd seen anything suspicious in recent weeks. I told him all about a man I'd seen and gave a full description; I got really into it. He took out a pad and pen and jotted down everything I was saying. I believe he took it all quite seriously and when I'd finished he asked if I would go down to the station with him to give a statement. I said my mother would never allow it and ran off. In bed that night I lay awake worrying I had inadvertently described someone who lived in the neighbourhood. I imagined them being arrested and convicted on the strength of the testimony of a child with nothing better to do with his time than lie to policemen.

We ran about the place collaring small children, telling them if they didn't watch it they'd go the same way as Susie Banshawe; then we worried one of them would cry and blab and we'd become the main suspects. Oh, why were we so cruel? We just did what older kids had done to us before, but that doesn't excuse it.

They found her of course, though it took three long weeks when all the adults were on edge and jumpy. She had been strangled and buried in a muddy plot of land at the edge of our estate. It was a foolish place to put her; the land was marked for building and she would have been discovered sooner or later, but I suppose the killer was in a panic and could think of nothing better. They never caught him, never even got close it seems. Mysteries aren't meant to be left unsolved, are they?

I say 'they' found her, but it was me. I found her. Jammy and I were playing along the disused rail track that ran alongside the estate. All the kids went down there. There was a gap in one of the hedges you could squeeze through and run across the muddy plot of land to get home if you were due home for tea and needed to get back quick. I had new wellies on and halfway across the muddy field my feet sank into the mud—one welly wedged solid. You'd think I was marooned in a cave with the tide coming in with the fuss I made, screaming the whole place down. Jammy laughed his head off and shouted his goodbyes, not wanting to be late; his father could be a bit of a lout. I cried hot, childish tears, which are the best kind to cry even in adult life. I stood there expecting the ground to swallow me up, though my foot had barely moved since I first wedged it there. I stood there in a field of mud and waved at the houses on the street opposite. Their windows regarded me like dead eyes: empty, indifferent. Nobody came. Nobody drove by. I suppose there were fewer cars then; we can all say that of our childhoods. I was alone there.

I didn't do well with being left alone. Once in a garden centre I lost sight of my parents. I had been weaving in and out of the little square flowerbeds, balancing as though on a tightrope strung across a canyon, and when I looked up my parents had gone. I trampled those perfectly formed flowerbeds, feeling the edges of my vision start to blur. I fell down on the pathway and everything went black. I remember sitting in the boot of the car, my legs dangling, and a woman came up to us and said, 'Oh dear, is it cancer?' What foolish things adults say.

I stood there, on that muddy patch of land, one boot stuck solid, and for a moment it went completely silent. When I first got married, my wife and I drove up a mountain in Cyprus and got out at the top and it was the most profound silence I had ever experienced. Theresa loved it. She said we should build a cabin there and never go back home, but all I could think about was being stuck in that field in my wellies.

My mum came eventually; it was probably only minutes. Jammy must have called her when he got home. She strode across that field with a smile on her face and asked why I hadn't just lifted my foot out of the welly. I hadn't even thought of it. I did just that and she pulled my boot out of the ground with a satisfying squelch. That night she got to thinking that the mud should have sucked me down, and she called the police. That's where they found Susie Banshawe, buried under my boot print.

Her mother came and watched them while they dug; I guess she knew the truth of it somehow. Her cries were so loud they etched on all our brain cells and I hope as I get older they'll be the first ones to go, but I know they won't.

Strangely, it was my father who wanted to move away and Mum who wanted to stay. All her friends were there, she said, and she'd just joined the badminton club. Chasing a ridiculously named piece of plastic twice a week seemed to be more important to her than the safety of her child. I thought briefly that Father's desire to leave was because he had finished Susie Banshawe off himself, but reasoned that if it were true, at least I was in no danger; if he killed his own child it would only draw unwanted attention his way. I don't think there was a man on the estate who people didn't wonder about, which looking back on it is the reason he wanted to leave I suppose. Their marriage was disintegrating then. Perhaps they hadn't really noticed yet, but a few years later and there was no concealing it. I didn't know it then, but when I first saw the cracks starting to show, I wasn't surprised. That's what the whole Susie Banshawe business taught me. I came to see I was always standing on the surface while something unsavoury lurked beneath.

And I tell you her name because I have never forgotten it. Susie Banshawe, Susie Banshawe. When that man did what he did to her he must have thought it would affect her family, that it would affect his own mind, may even have thought of his own family's feelings in the event he was caught. But he won't have thought of a boy running across a muddy field in his new wellies. He won't have considered the effect it would have on me.

They built houses on that field, just as they had planned to. There was talk of a commemorative garden or something, but she'd been dumped off-centre and it spoiled the plans to change the design. Besides, who wanted to buy a new house overlooking a garden in memory of some murdered kid?

We watched the houses go up, but Jammy and I never poked around in those skulls, never jumped out of windows there. We were solemn onlookers. So was Susie Banshawe's mother. She did move away, but she kept coming back, a familiar sight over the years, just standing and watching. Once when Jammy and I stood there, a car sped by and one of its hubcaps came off and spun down the road, weaving uncertainly like Mr Pope from number thirty-two on the way back from the pub, finally stopping and doing that thing kids try to do with anything disc shaped and metal: spinning round and round and then clank-clank-clanking against the ground until it stopped. There were long, long seconds of silence then, before Jammy and I hooted with laughter. We howled, we were so happy. It lightened the tone, took away the tension. Jammy took the hubcap home and hung it in his room. His dad humoured him for a week then threw it away or sold it on, who knows.

Now people stand there and say, 'Before there were houses, this was all fields', all knowing and solemn like there used to be concrete slabs where their houses were built. 'Before there were houses, this was all fields.' But you can say that about anywhere, can't you? We all live on old fields, hills, ancient countryside. They even got together to sign a petition to stop the next lot of houses that went up; then the people who moved in there joined in on the petition for the next lot and so it went on. When I'm in bed in my room it's still four walls around me; makes no differ-ence how far the houses stretch down the street. No one stands there and says, 'Before there were houses, a girl was strangled and buried there', because it would be unfeeling to the people who have moved in.

I still live on the estate now. I look at those houses, on that ground where my boot print located a dead girl and I think,

'Before I was this, I was something else, something less cluttered.'

We're all something before other things get built on top, things that push down or obscure what was first there. Before we were houses, we were all fields. I think about myself stuck in that field in my new wellingtons, thinking if I had sunk below the mud I would have sunk right into Susie Banshawe. That thought has kept me awake some nights, I can tell you. And always her mother, standing on the street opposite those houses, in the same way I was with my boots, as if her slightly scuffed black flats have sunk into the tarmac, held her fast, and she is waiting for rescue.

———

She was not yet ready to let go of her childhood. It was cruel of her father to gather her old toys up when she was out and throw them away.

She shed her tears in private, not wishing him to see how this had hurt her. She wanted to keep just one thing back—a wooden elephant on wheels. This is what she would have chosen. Just one item, a memento. A token to remind her who she had been, how she had felt.

She wondered how this toy could be rescued and remembered how she watched the other children play with the dustbin trucks each Wednesday. She did not like the smell of rotten food. She did not like the men, with their fluorescent clothes, their dirty hands, and filthy faces. But she wished to recover her wooden elephant on wheels.

She waited down the side of her house. When the dustman came to pick up the sacks of rubbish at the end of her drive she asked him if he had seen her toy.

'You should come back to my place sometime,' he said. 'The things I find that people throw out, you wouldn't believe.'

He scribbled the address on a scrap of paper and pressed it into her hand.

'What is your name?' he said.

'Susan,' she said. 'But don't tell anyone I spoke to you. I don't want my father to know.'

His house had a sheen of dirt across it as if it worked the dust carts alongside him. Inside you could hardly move. Things were piled up everywhere. She wrinkled her nose at the smell.

'Drink this,' he said, handing her a glass that smelled of the drinks at the back of her father's cabinet. 'I make it myself.'

He showed her some of the things he had rescued from the teeth of his truck. He could see the value of things that were lost, were thrown away, could find some wonder in every item. She felt he too was looking for something he had lost.

All around her the room began to sway. Light reflected from a myriad metal objects until she felt a million little stars were shining just for her.

Woodwork trains began to trundle along the shelves. Teddy bears clutched at the stuffing bursting from their sides and pushed it back in, their cheeks burning with shame.

And in the corner of the room, an elephant on wheels raised its trunk and let out a mighty trumpeting sound.

2

A GIANT EMERGES

HE WAS IN THE LOFT, drilling down through the ceiling. She balanced on a ladder below, marking the points his drill bit burst through. The dust rained down, a mini waterfall, into her eyes. I like you this way, she thought. I like the idea of you. A disembodied voice. You are the dream of a husband I once had and remember fondly. She imagined locking the loft hatch, trying to keep him this way; knowing he would kick his way through the plasterboard ceiling, a foot emerging in a cloud of dust, a giant coming down from the skies.

3

—————

FEATHERING

THERE IS A FEATHERING OF SNOW, your mother says, and to her this is something slight, inconsequential. To you, though, this would be enough. Each snowflake could blister your skin, causing you pain. You stand at the window and watch the flakes fall—so innocent—stare hard at them until your eyes blur. You watch them catch and swirl in the wind and wonder if the wind blew hard enough whether you could navigate a path between the snowflakes so they would not touch your skin. You picture them as tiny white butterflies, too timid to land on you. You would walk amongst them then and lose yourself in this flurry of blankness falling from above.

But you are indoors, where you must be. You are the disease, and the disease is you. There is no walking away from it; it makes itself known at all times. It has a name, and it is a proper medical name. One that is long with more consonants than seems possible. There is a three letter abbreviation, but you prefer the name in all its glory. Once you have mastered the shape of the syllables you use this full name. Three letters will not do—they do not convey the magnitude of this thing. Three letters are given to shops, to diggers, to flippant things. There are twenty-four consonants and ten vowels in this medical name, and you turn them over in your mouth, feeling the shape of them. The o and c are safest—you can roll them around—but the blunt edges of the k can do you harm. Sometimes you say it as if it were a complicated job title or a qualification, something you would be proud to have.

'Where shall we go today?' your mother says.

She does these things because this is what would happen in a movie version of your life. There would be edited cuts of the happy things you do, the times when you are laughing together. It would not show the moments when someone knocks against you and you shriek in pain, or when something is spilled and your skin blisters. These are just the moments in between. Uplifting music soars and you both laugh. This is what you do together; you search out these moments, but without the music. Your mother is edgy and flustered. Her sister is visiting from Australia, with her son. It is three years since they have seen each other.

'What if we have nothing to talk about?' your mother says.

'Sisters always have something to talk about,' you reply.

It is January and the Christmas decorations are back in their gloomy box in the loft but you are still listening to the carols. You have been told it's bad luck to listen to them, but you give what your mother calls 'one of your withering looks' and you are allowed to carry on, though your mother says, 'You can always have more bad luck.'

You hum them now as you walk into the shopping centre. Your favourite is O Holy Night because this is a joke in your family: it features the line 'a thrill of hope, the weary world rejoices'. At this the family cheer.

'What can we say?' your father says. 'We are thrilled by you.'

You and your mother wander around the shops. You get looks; you always get looks. Sometimes you drop your gaze to the ground and ignore the stares. Other times you play up to it, pulling your most gruesome face. Most times you walk along and it is just part of your day, this being looked at. Your mother buys a cardigan for her sister and a jumper for Josh.

'It's summer over there,' she says. 'They'll probably be freezing when they get here.'

You buy a newspaper too, because a man came to the house to talk to you and he has shared what you said with the world, or at least the people in the world who read this paper. You do not know how you feel about this.

———

Back at home you have lunch and your mother barely eats a thing. Your sisters are in their best dresses and your father has tried to keep them from running wild and spoiling them. They are excited, poring over the pictures in the newspaper and laughing at their expressions.

'You're famous, Hope,' they say. 'Aren't you excited?'

'I'm in the paper because there's something wrong with me,' you say, 'and now everyone who reads it will know my business.'

Later, there is a knock at the door and you all gather, positioning yourselves as if you are posing for a family portrait, which in some sense you are. Your mother brushes down the sides of her dress, though there are no creases and it fits her perfectly. She steps forward and opens the door. The woman there is a version of your mother, tanned and muscular, happier, and it surprises you, though you have seen her before and know they look alike. Your cousin Josh is barely recognisable. He is a young man now. He smiles sweetly and shakes the hands that are offered to him. He looks you in the eye and nods to you, without extending his hand. He has, of course, remembered his freakish cousin. He is prepared. But he doesn't stare. His eyes flick away from you.

Your mother and aunt have found things to talk about. They have not stopped talking. Everyone else is listening to what they have to say to each other. You know your mother has harboured hopes of joining her sister in Australia, but it is not practical.

'It's too hot for Hope,' your mother says. 'It's not safe. Her skin blisters.'

You feel your skin redden enough to blister and wish it was not necessary to talk about you in this way.

———

You have an unhealthy obsession (your mother's words) with martyrs; a poster of Joan of Arc is pinned above your bed. You see the irony, of course, but you also feel the first agony of searing pain as the flames flicker and caress the skin. She is there to show you that things could be much worse. You have, too, a fascination with fire. When your father piles logs in the fireplace you watch and wait for the first glow as the wood begins to burn. You fashion little paper people out of twisted toilet tissue and throw them into the flames. On your good days, when your skin is calm, you reach out your hand and think of pushing it against the burning wood, because sometimes the anticipation of the pain to come is worse than the pain itself.

It is late at night but your mother and her sister are still up. There is laughter and what sounds like crying, but you resist the urge to sit halfway down the stairs and eavesdrop as you used to. You could never hear anything anyway, and more often than not were caught by your father, who knew never to talk when he was on his way to the door, not giving you time to scarper back up the stairs. You lean against your door frame and when you look up, Josh is standing in the doorway of the spare room watching you. He comes and stands with you and you wonder what you look like beside each other. You are pale in comparison to this boy, in every way.

Because he is close family, but not too close, you tell him things you have been unable to say before. You tell him you are jealous of your two younger sisters, who can run and play with no fear, who sunbathe in the summer and whose skin is clear, but that you cannot imagine life without them. They always treat you with love and include you in their games when they can. You tell him of the things you have read in books and online about your condition, words that settle in your heart and fester, keeping you awake at night. You cry in front of this boy and he holds your hand, forgetting what this may do. It hurts, but you don't mind at all.

In the morning your mother treats your skin. She pricks the blisters so they will not grow, wiping away the fluid that follows. She peels back the skin that has started to flake, and rubs ointment in as gently as she can. You scream; you always scream. However much you wish to be brave, you scream. She binds your hands and pushes your gloves on. This is your routine and you do not talk, either of you. Your mother used to chatter away until one day you cried and asked for it to be done in silence. This time at the end your mother smiles. Sometimes there are tears in her eyes, but not today.

'Pick a nice dress,' she says. 'Josh is taking you out.'

'Where?' you say, feeling flustered and embarrassed and important all at once.

'He won't say,' she says. 'It's a surprise. I'm not too sure about it all myself but your dad says you're to go, so there you are.'

He drives slowly and you try to guess where you are going. You suppose it will be to the cinema, but you pass the turn leading that way and the minutes pass. On the motorway he asks you to close your eyes.

'It's a surprise,' he says. 'No peeking. You can trust me.'

You don't peek, because this is fun and you do not want to ruin the surprise.

When you get out of the car you hear an elephant trumpet. You are at the zoo, or the circus.

'Are you throwing me to the lions? Is this what it's come to?' you say.

You hear him laugh and you smile.

He calls out instructions, lefts and rights and mind the steps, and is careful not to guide you with a hand on your arm or back, which could damage your skin. You are cold, but your clothes have to be loose, and it is better to be cold than crying. You try not to show you are frightened you may stumble. You put your faith in this boy who is joined to you through blood. You are inside then and you hear Josh pull aside a plastic curtain. You smell strange things and hear children and grown men crying out, saying 'waah' and 'Oh my God'. Josh leans over and whispers in your ear.

'You can look now,' he says.

You are in a bat cave. It makes you sound like a super hero. Free flying Egyptian fruit bats, the sign says. Do not worry, it says, they are unlikely to fly into you. You focus on the word unlikely, but do not want to show Josh that you are scared. Your eyes adjust to the dark quickly, having been shut for so long. You are proud you didn't peek. The bats whizz across the room. There are slow clicking noises that speed up when the bats approach. There is a night vision camera, and on the wall is a TV screen where you can see yourself and the shapes flying around you.

'Echo-location,' says Josh, reading from a poster. 'That's why they don't hit you.'

There is a feathering, a breeze, a rush on your skin as the bats fly past you. You laugh, and yelp, you scream and cry a little, and for a moment, for many moments, you feel at one with your name.

4

LITTLE YELLOW SQUARES

THEY SIT OPPOSITE EACH OTHER, shoulders slumped, this father and this son. The similarities are there, if you choose to look: around the eyes, the thinness of the upper lip, the slump of the shoulders. Life has treated them both the same way, though they don't care to admit it, to themselves or to each other.

They are in the kitchen. Around them, on walls, utensils, appliances, sit little yellow squares, as if they have been disturbed doing something they shouldn't; they cling to whatever is nearest so as not to be noticed. The father would rather not notice them. Across each of them a single word, a lesson his son is trying to teach him. I am not an idiot, the father says when he is at his most lucid. I know, his son says, his patience thin.

They sit in silence; it has often been this way between them. What colour is your anger, the son says sometimes. Red, the father says, thinking of things that are angry and red. He does not say them aloud, but his son is ready for them. He has read all the right books. There is hardness in his father's eyes that he remembers from his boyhood. I'll teach you a lesson you'll never forget, his father would say, and the boy would run. Never fast enough, or far enough. The father remembers these things too.

A fluttering noise breaks the silence between them, a movement that catches in the right eye of the father and the left eye of the son. They turn together. The little yellow square on the coffee percolator has folded itself in half and is flapping its two halves back and forth. The father and the son both watch this silently. It launches itself into the air, hovers momentarily, then swoops around them.

A rustling, a muted round of applause then, as all the little yellow squares test their newfound wings. Then there is a blur of little yellow squares around them, like blossoms falling. They are surrounded like this for perhaps a minute, then the little yellow squares find a place to land and fold themselves flat again. I hope they have landed correctly, the son thinks. I have not shown my son enough moments of joy, the father thinks.

The father and the son turn to stare at each other, their eyes aglow at the wonder they have shared. The father puts his finger on the pad of sticky notes that sits on the table between them. He slides it to him and writes on it. He covers the note with his hands for a moment.

When he releases it, the little yellow square he has written on folds itself in half, launches into the air, turns an attractive spiral and lands on the father's forehead. Its two halves remain closed for several beats, twitching slightly. When it opens its wings the son looks at his father, his eyes filling with long suppressed tears.

5

WE SINK WHEN WE SWIM

HE SWIMS NOW, back and forth, at night. Nothing special, just the breast stroke—it is all he can do. He panics when he puts his foot down, has misjudged it and there is nothing there.

He steps out from the conservatory. The plastic doors warp in the heat, cracking and groaning their displeasure, and do not shut easily. He wrestles with them until he hears them click.

Moonlight brushes his skin and he looks down to see how brightly he is lit, the folds of his flesh are desert hills moving from light to shade. He pads across the patio, hoping not to hear the crunch of a snail underfoot, or to feel the squelch of a slug. This has happened before. It was like stepping into the warmth of freshly expelled dog shit. He could wear slippers, but the thrill of the nudity is gone with slippers.

He presses the button and the covers roll back. The plastic scrape of them against the sides is amplified in the night air and if the neighbours are out perhaps they will peer through gaps in the conifers to see what is happening. But, it is late and they are unlikely to be outside. If they should look, it is too dark to make out whether he is wearing anything or not. The thrill of his nakedness is only there with the certainty he will not be seen.

When the cover rolls back completely he does not pause. He slips off the side and into the water. The pool is not heated. It is always cold at first. He has learned to walk to the edge of the deep end and get straight under. To delay for only a moment can lead to minutes of indecision. If his teeth are gritted tight together and there is an intake of breath, then it is not too bad.

He finds the peace that eludes him in the daytime. He concentrates on the rhythm of his crude strokes, the kick of his feet in the water, the whiff of chlorine tickling the inside of his nose.

He swims as he has always swum. He is all the places he has ever swum.

He is a boy, sitting in a paddling pool, the water only a few inches deep. His mother watches from the window, or sits by him on a garden chair. He splashes the water with his hands and is happy.

He is in the school swimming pool, a mass of floats and arm bands. His mother does not watch now, but there are teachers with whistles at each end of the pool. A girl in his year is pulled unconscious from the water when she hits her head on the side. She laughs about it later and there is a bump on her forehead for weeks.

He is at the local sports centre. He has never lost his reserve for changing into swimwear, perfected on many beach holidays as a child: wrapping a towel around his waist and fumbling with his underwear and trunks—so undignified. Here men have it all hanging out, rows of them at the showers, passing idle conversation as they soap themselves as if they are at a bar ordering drinks. In time he learns to dispense with the towel, but everything is done in one swift motion when he is certain nobody is looking.

He is his past. It is hard not to slip into it when he swims back and forth. Never sure enough to swim freely, there is always some concentration involved, but part of his mind is free to wander, and it is more tempting to arrive back in the past than to ponder the mundane aspects of his present life, or to think about what he has done.

He can will himself back, to anywhere, to the sports centre. The walls he builds up around him, that cavernous chamber, and the sides of the garden stretch away. He was young then; he spent his time running and cycling to improve his physique so he did not feel ashamed in his trunks.

It was unpleasant the way the screams of children echoed in there, the hollow ring of parents calling. No matter how high the ceilings it could never pass for outside. He had never learned to swim properly, or pushed himself to build the strength required to swim one lap of a swimming pool after another; he had not really progressed much beyond the paddling pool.

There were classes held each day, but he was too embarrassed to join them. Instead he patiently swam from the shallow end to the deep end, hoping nobody would block his way. He could not stop, unable to tread water. At each end he waited a few seconds, then started back the way he had come. She was beside him one day in the deep end when he reached out his fingers for the edge, always a little too early, a little too desperately. They found they had things they wished to say to each other.

She married an image of him that was then not there. He had no sympathy for her. She had seen him at the pool, swimming in his ponderous way, while others glided through the water, sending ripples her way. She should have known. In the wedding photos he stood fiddling with his shirtsleeves, hands shaking, stomach shifting. Had she seen it then, sifting through them, looking for one to frame and hang in the hallway? In the end she chose one of her father helping her from the car—their wedding photo and he was not even in it.

In the flower beds the solar lanterns phase through their colours and he watches the effect the different shades have on the conifer hedges. In the house the lights are on in one of the bedrooms so he has light to see by. In this subdued light he can only make out shapes. He weaves his way in and out of them, happy to swim through leaves but hoping to miss the beetles, the woodlice, the spiders.

Just below the surface, faded carcasses of insects, pale and see-through, shadows of what they once were, brush against his skin, no more than the touch of the water. And further below… He does not think about this. Do not think about this.

But the mind, oh, the mind is not so easily fooled. He thinks then of a boy, a boy who begged his father to go up in a hot-air balloon, a boy who pleaded, who pulled at his father's sleeves and whined until he relented. A boy who regretted his decision as soon as the ground swung away from him. His father's hand across his shoulders. 'Just breathe. Look straight ahead. Don't look down.'

Don't look down. Don't look down.

He did not expect to own a house with a swimming pool, but when they looked for something in their price range, there it was. It didn't seem to have added anything to the price.

'They eat money if you heat them,' the young estate agent said, leafing through his notes as if he were looking for things he could be blamed for later. 'It puts people off if they do their research.'

He didn't do his research. The pool and the garden sold it for him, while his wife loved the inside of the house, in her mind had it decorated to her standards before they had even stepped out into the garden and seen the pool.

She was not enamoured by water and swam only for her health. In truth she was a little scared by it, though she liked to visit lakes or the sea, as if taking herself to the brink of danger. In the same way she climbed tall buildings and towers then hung back from the edge. She peered over the glass floor at Blackpool Tower as if it were an open void that could suck her through. She edged around the Eiffel Tower as if gravity worked both horizontally and vertically.

When they settled into the house, she was as attracted as he with the idea of a swimming pool in their garden, imagining it as a backdrop to summer barbecues and picnics, then when they realised how much money it took to keep it running, she drew in a breath and declared they would 'get their money's worth'.

Neither of them were strong swimmers, both red faced with the effort of getting from one end to the other without stopping, neither able to tread water, however much they tried.

'There is a trick to it they are not telling us,' she would say, with no hint of a smile and no indication of who 'they' may be.

She told him he could not go in when she wasn't with him.

'I've no wish to come home and find you floating face down,' she warned, fearful of heart attacks, asthma attacks, alien attacks —who knew what. Why these things would be any more palatable on dry land, he didn't know, but he nodded and agreed to it. When she was out he wound the cover back and sat on the edge with his legs dangling and thought about getting in, always convincing himself that it felt a bit too cold, or he wasn't in the mood.

'She will come home early if you do get in,' a voice whispered in his head, and this was the real reason he didn't jump in.

She liked the pool to be there in the background, but did not like to talk about it. She was ashamed of her fears, embarrassed to have not improved her strokes. She laughed it off when asked.

'We never use it much,' she said. 'We sink when we swim.'

If he narrows his eyes the lashes meet, reproduce the shapes of people, parties on the patio, gatherings they had, mostly her friends, clutching at glasses of wine and waiting to leave, the pool as backdrop.

'We like the neighbours on our left,' she would say at these gatherings, and there were nods of agreement. Though he knew who she meant, of course, he could never understand how anybody else did. Were the neighbours on the left ascertained as one approached the house, or as one stood on the doorstep and faced outward? It was just one of the many trivial rules of life he had not been taught, as if he had misplaced an imaginary handbook.

The neighbours on one side, 'to the right' he supposed, built an extension resembling a warehouse on the side of their property soon after they moved in, making it feel as if they had taken an aggressive step toward them.

'You must complain,' she said, but part of him rather liked this being hemmed in, this further reduction of the outside world, and he was pleased the pool could no longer be seen from the neighbours' upstairs windows.

Everything on the surface, round and round, twigs and insects wriggling. He wants to stretch out his arms and follow them round. His memories circulate, edging ever closer to the filter, pulling away from him.

They didn't know how to look after a swimming pool. There were plastic pipes and levers leading to a rusting boiler, all this in a small room outside, festooned with spiders. He learned how to filter the water round, but the boiler stuttered to a halt after a couple of years and, though it shortened their 'season', as they laughingly called it, they did not fix it.

One year they left the summer cover on into winter and the water turned green. No amount of chlorine would shift the fetid clouds that appeared when they swept the brush along the bottom.

In dreams he still swims these fetid swirls, the whirr of insects skim the surface, lily pads bloom, a crocodile's tail follows lazily behind him.

They were forced to drain all the water and scrub the tiles until the mould was gone, each tile becoming slippery so they slid back down into the deep end each time they tried to climb their way back up the slope. Once, when he slipped, he knocked her with him, and they landed in a bedraggled heap at the bottom, his glasses falling and the side arm jabbing into his eye, blood pooling on the newly cleaned tiles.

She was obsessed then with the chlorine levels, not wishing to repeat this exercise, matching the dipstick against the chart and shaking her head. He threw two large chlorine pellets in each week and was done with it. They looked like giant Refreshers and he imagined fizzing them on his tongue and how clean his mouth would feel after.

Still things failed. The tiles fell and had to be fished from the bottom before they slipped into the filter. She used them as decorations on the flowerbeds once it became obvious that his promises to re-stick them would go unfulfilled.

Ants crawled out from the patio around the pool and some of the slabs began to sink. He put down ant killer though he hated to kill anything, but they came back year after year. When the heat was right in the summer the pool was dusted with a covering of flying ants and he wondered what instinct made them land there when they were meant to be looking for somewhere to nest.

Despite this they swum once a day, when the sun, if it was out, was at its highest. Without the boiler the water could be icy, particularly if the nights had been cold.

'I think if I were not so afraid of the water,' she said, 'I would be the sort to swim in the sea all year through. It really is bracing.'

Bracing. As if this was a positive thing, when it could also mean to prepare for something unpleasant.

Images were taken from above of the house and garden because everything must be seen somewhere these days, and on one they were both there, on the surface of the pool, two insects wriggling, until one day the site was updated and they disappeared.

———

He thinks of her now and this way conjures her back into existence, raises her vertical again, sets her moving, his own automaton version of her that he can manipulate within the scope of his own memories. He cannot make her what she was not, but he can avoid what she is now.

When the night sky is clear he feels he may be lifted from the water, he feels the opposite of gravity ushering him toward the stars. He thinks of a man in a pool on another planet looking at the pinprick of light that shows where he is, and he imagines the distance between them.

Yes, his life is in here, round and round. Age has made him comfortable with the flailing, wild strokes he has always had. He concentrates on what lies on the surface, the feel of his naked body moving through the water.

And below... below... He ignores the dark mass below, which is much more than pine needles, decaying leaves, and moss.

———

Their three children had swam away from his wife far too early, too soon even to tell if they were male or female. This means he cannot picture who they would be now.

'We fail at all the big things,' his wife said.

He knows he has avoided much in his life, but had he not been married he would not have seen this as a failure. He thinks of his father, working machines in an engineering factory his whole life, the dust, the grime. His mother, cleaning toilets and worse. He has a house with a pool. He does not think this to brag, just to show that in some ways he has not failed.

He brought home a leaflet from the local library on adoption and placed it on the sideboard in the hallway one morning when he left for work. He wanted to show her that he was not precious about his bloodline, that the doors were not all closed. When he got home the leaflet was gone and she did not mention it. He looked for it crumpled in a bin, but it was nowhere to be found.

One thing he cannot conjure up in here is the swell and sway of the sea. (Though the fear of what lies beneath, yes, he has a little of that.) They had holidayed once in Cyprus, spending their time at a secluded beach divided by two lines of rocks from the shore out to sea. Despite his lack of swimming prowess he had been drawn by the challenge of the rocky outcrop.

Setting off all seemed fine; there were few other swimmers to get in his way, and though the distance was further than the length of a pool he thought he could make it. Then he began to imagine all sorts coming at him from the depths, or heading his way from the endless expanse ahead of him. When he reached the other shore he felt he had conquered new land. That section of beach was louder, playful. There was a bar selling food, music lilting from its open doors. He clambered over the rocks back to his wife with a wistful look over his shoulder before making the final jump down.

He tried things over the years to better himself: ill-conceived business ventures and inventions. Later in life there were programs on television where you could present such ideas before a panel of experts. One night, watching this together, she said, 'Back in the day you would have gone on this,' and as he smiled and nodded she said, 'and we would have had to move.' After that he could see how he would be the jokey one or the ridiculous one shoehorned in between those whose pitches were successful.

They stayed in Portugal one year—their own private villa. They swam and splashed about in the pool for the first couple of days trying not to comment on its pristine tiling, spotless boiler room, and the level slabs surrounding it. Then the couple staying in the villa next door introduced themselves, and clung like the spiders that cluttered their boiler room at home.

Their villa did not have a pool, could they use theirs? The man had a toned torso and swam like a professional, pounding the water with his arms, racing up and down for endless minutes. In the face of this he and his wife could do no more than sit by the pool for the rest of the holiday, marvelling at the ability of some people to intrude on others.

She did not wish to fly after seeing the towers fall and they were reduced to weekends away in their own country, taking a chance on the sun joining them.

She was the one constant in his life, telling him what he could and couldn't do. She was his cautionary lifeguard, sounding the whistle before he had a chance to get into trouble. He wonders now if there was one swallowed retort that signalled the way things would be, or if she had won a string of arguments and he had backed off. It is hard to remember. They seemed always to have been the same way.

He suffers from bloating in later life and something about the stretch of his body in the water eases this and he takes delight in the ripple of bubbles he can produce, something she most certainly would not have approved of.

In the breeze the beach ball he uses as a float when he is tired skitters across the water to him with something like enthusiasm and he half smiles at it as if it were an eager puppy come to have its ears tickled.

A vein bubbles, sending a ripple under the surface of the skin, an echo of his own external one in the pool, but this is not amusing, the way his body betrays him.

If she had held him back in any way it is hard to see how since he has carried on as before without her. It is not as if his life is over. He is, after all, still strong enough to swim. But there is more behind than ahead. Perhaps there will be sports centre swimming pools again, this time on special days with people his age, where he can't be splashed or forced out the way. Then perhaps it will be the bath into which he will be lowered by some kind of contraption, a mess of pulleys and buttons as his father had been reduced to.

He can feel the pull of what is below, though he tries to avoid it. All this time he has been conscious of the dark shapes beneath him. It is useless to pretend. He takes a breath and plunges his head below.

Down here with the dim underwater light he is a boy again, back in his school swimming lessons. He is embarrassed by the changes in his body, the hair that grows, and he walks to school in his trunks, dawdles home at the end of the day with a wet patch spreading. But this is the bit he likes, pinching his nose and sinking underwater. The joy of opening his eyes and seeing the legs and arms of the boys and girls thrashing through the water around him.

Standing on the bottom, it is like he has reached a place no one else will ever reach. But he is not there now and the dark mass below him is nothing he wishes to see. He shuts his eyes and when his head starts to pound with the pressure of holding his breath he counts to ten... twenty... thirty.

He looks into the light.

It flickers. She never let him put it on, unable to understand how a light could be safe underwater. It does not work well but he can see all that is laid out beneath him.

These are the items he has been unable to face, left in the house alone: photographs, jewellery, the mementos bought, the trinkets she had gathered, her shoes, hats, all the things on show. Still her closed drawers and cupboards taunt him. He feels the weight from the loft above, half expecting the hatch to burst open at any minute. He had gathered as much as he could, filled black bags and, unable to think clearly, emptied them into the pool, tears pouring.

Oh, how he had loved her.

In one of the photographs she is smiling and her arm is outstretched. She is reaching for the camera, wanting to take his picture. He opens a hand toward her now. He is feeling light-headed. He places his feet down on all that is there and pushes back up to the surface. He draws in breaths, clinging to the beach ball and staring at the gloom below.

The chlorine will fade these things and he will replace them. There are many more things, packed away. It will be a pleasure and a pain to rediscover them.

He gets out and wraps a towel around, feeling the water drip down the inside of his legs. He winds the cover back, pulling the rope to help it on its way, steering it left and right when it goes astray.

When he gets into bed and closes his eyes, if he can still feel the rocking motion of the water, still see her reaching out to him, then he is happy.

6

____

BUTTERFLY FARM

SHE WISHED to work with butterflies because she found them beautiful. I will surround myself with their colours, she thought, then I shall be happy. It will give me some meaning in my life.

She interviewed at the butterfly farm, armed with all the salient facts, neatly copied onto cards in her pocket. She had adored butterflies in books and fluttering prettily in her garden. But up close she found they resembled tiny, crumpled alien men and she would shudder at the sight of them. They are like the men I have let into my heart, she thought. Stooped and devious. She turned away from them and wrote out her notice on the back of one of her interview cards.

She felt she owed them an explanation for her swift departure so she found the smallest, most colourful butterfly and poured out her heart.

In the park she sat with her back to the butterfly farm and wondered why she was denied happiness. A tree across from her stood bare-branched and sad and she found she could not look away from it. That tree is my life, she thought. Empty. A great sadness overtook her.

Though there was no discernible breeze she could hear one behind her. Above her then a dark cloud as hundreds of butterflies escaped the farm and alighted on the branches of the tree, gently flapping their wings, giving the impression of leaves undulating.

7

―――――――――――――

THIS BIRD SHE CALLS FEAR

THROUGH THE FROSTED glass she sees him standing there on the doorstep. She recognises his silhouette at once. He is thinner than ever, but he holds himself in the same way, and the shape of his head is the same.

She steadies herself against the door frame, fingers clenched tight. The bird she calls fear flutters its wings within her chest. This is the moment she has hoped for and dreaded in equal measure. She does not know if she is strong enough.

She felt the first tremors of fear as he left for France when the fighting began. She could see through his bluster that he felt the same, but they did not speak of it. To name it out loud would be to jinx him in some way. And so he went, and she tried to contain it within herself. As black-edged letters began to be delivered in the village, the fear felt so strong she thought she would stop breathing altogether.

The fear that lay within her had sat in her stomach like bad food. She could see no future for herself without this unease, this sickness within her belly. It felt like the early stages of pregnancy, like saying her marriage vows in front of a packed church. She had done all she could to remove herself from it: focusing on tasks, counting to one hundred, reasoning with herself that all would be well, but it was no use. She began to think of it as a bird; to think of it this way made her feel it was something she could steady, could soothe somehow. She would rub her hand across her stomach whispering 'hush now', as she had done when her children were growing inside her.

In this way she learned to control her fears. She let the bird turn a few times within her stomach, make itself at home, settle down, make a nest. If it was going to be there she wished it to make itself comfortable.

So, to settle the bird she prepared herself to lose him. It was inevitable, the law of averages. It could not be avoided. She was always waiting for her black-edged letter. The pain would be lessened if she readied herself for it. It had been the only way to combat the fear, to still the bird. But in preparing herself to lose him she feared now that she had indeed lost him, had imagined a life without him too well, spent too long without him. Now she does not know if they can get back what they had.

She pauses with her hand on the door handle while he shuffles his feet. A cobweb hangs listlessly above the door frame and she wonders whether she should have hung streamers. There is the smell of polish in the air, though it is some days since she last cleaned. She opens the door.

This is not the first time she has seen him since he left. There has been leave and those visits had been easy. They had both play acted at their lives, playing them out as they had been before the war broke.

She'd had three children from those visits. Tommy, Jean, and little Harold, who'd not made it through his first week.

'Maybe he saw the world and didn't think it worth living in,' he wrote when she told him. She did not know what to do with these dark moods.

He smiles, and the smile does not reach his eyes. She reaches in to kiss him and the kiss is awkward, too formal. She can smell the hours of travel on him and pulls back from this.

She gestures him in and he stands in the hallway after she has shut the door, as if he needs permission to enter further into his own house.

She looks at him. Who is this man? she thinks. There was a man like him, before the war, a man with whom she had petty little arguments about the muddy footprints he brought in, or the way he ate the dinner she made without thanking her. This was not that man.

They sit in the front room and look at each other. The bird is flying circles around her internal organs. This house, this room has never felt so small. He is wearing his uniform. She thinks he will want to take it off, asks him if he wishes to change, but he insists on leaving it on. He rubs his hand up and down his legs as if trying to brush something off, to rub away some remembered stain. Was he given a new uniform to return home in? She does not know, is too afraid to ask. Rather than test out what is acceptable to talk about she prefers to keep silent.

'We should go for a walk,' he says, and she nods in agreement, glad for the idea of fresh air and space.

Outside the smell of summer is inside her nose, hot and heavy. She walks beside him, feeling the weight of her hands by her side. They always walked hand in hand before, through the village, across the fields, and his friends would call out and jeer in jest. But she finds herself to his right and does not want to move. He stops then, as if reading her thoughts, and she feels her face flush, suddenly, quickly. She fears she may fall. He looks at her for a moment.

'You have not changed,' he says, smiling, the curve of his mouth still not quite reaching his eyes, but getting nearer now, ever nearer. She places a hand on his cheek.

'And you are much changed,' she whispers.

He nods, and the tears gather on his lower eyelid. He quickly wipes them away. They walk on, and she longs to feel the nothingness that summer air brought before the war, that calm feeling that nothing is required of you. Tears spring to her eyes at the thought of all the time they have lost. She can see, too, in the blank spaces behind his eyes all that he has lost—friends, innocence, and things he may never be able to put into words, even for her.

A plastic beaker lies in the undergrowth, full of water from overnight rain. He stops beside it. A dead fly floats upside down on the surface of the water. He watches it rock gently in the breeze. She cannot begin to imagine what is going through his mind. But he is home now, home too soon, but he is home. He sniffs, looks ahead, and they carry on their way.

The bird likes to move about. She was foolish to think it would leave as soon as he returned home. She can feel it beating its wings against her heart, feels the fluttering motion against her chest. She looks at him suddenly, and knows they may not find the connection they had again. Perhaps it has been too long; perhaps too much has happened. She feels the bird dive and hit the pit of her stomach. It sits there, motionless, a heavy weight making her want to heave. She is forced to stop as she waits for the nausea to pass.

'You should walk this side,' he says, indicating his left with a nod of his head. 'So you can hold my hand.'

They walk on. His hand feels rough in hers, not how she remembers it. But the feeling in her heart is the same; how it feels to be held by him has not changed.

She kneels and picks a dandelion, smiling as she does so. She spins it around between her thumb and forefinger, places it in her buttonhole. She once said to him it was her favourite flower.

'It is nothing more than a weed,' he had said, laughing.

Once they had spent an afternoon with him calling her Dandy and her calling him Lion. She had often remembered that afternoon.

He reaches out to touch the dandelion in her buttonhole. She smiles at him.

'You have not asked to see the tattoo,' he says then.

He had got a tattoo, he wrote from the front; he did not know what she would think of that. She has not asked, fearful it had been on the right arm he had lost. She had pictured it laying there in the trenches, with her name inked on it perhaps, as if it belonged to her. She imagined it parcelled up and returned to her with a note: 'This must be yours, it has your name on it.' He pulls up the sleeve of his shirt and shows her his tattoo. She looks at him.

She takes the dandelion from her buttonhole and holds it against the one inked on his arm. Here is a moment she can stay in forever. The bird is quiet. For a moment the bird is quiet.

8

———————

MY FENCE IS ELECTRIC

SHE HAD NOT HAD good experiences with love, so she bought the wire and wound it around her heart as a barrier. It was true that it caused her considerable pain, but it was a constant pain—a hurt she was in control of.

When he met her he paid no attention to it, clambering over the wire and straight into her heart.

'Did you not see the fence I put up?' she said.

'Of course,' he said. 'I thought you had put a wall up against the outside world for us to live inside.'

She stared at him for a while, wondering if he was really so sure of himself, or just foolish, or both.

'I have one too,' he said. 'A fence. My fence is electric.'

It was the right thing to say. She let herself into his heart and, as she did so, she felt the tingle pulsing through her skin.

9

ROSA & THIRKEL

ROSA WOKE to the sound of hammer and nail, hammer and nail. Eyes tight shut, she listened, waiting for the curse words she knew would come. There... there was one; as a nail bent, as the hammer missed and jarred along his arm, as he thwacked his thumb—she did not know which of these it was. She slid a hand beneath her mattress, retrieving a slip of paper and pen, and marked a line next to the swear she'd heard. It was her father's third most popular, though she could see they were all well used. She had not added a new word to the list for some weeks now. This was a disappointment to her.

Outside the air was close, even at this early hour, fitting around her shoulders like a shawl. Bone dry earth skittered across the yard in the barest of breezes. They lived away from everything, Rosa and her father Thirkel. Only field and forest in all directions, a haze of greens and browns when she narrowed her eyes.

Thirkel saw her. He put the wood down, shielding his eyes from the sun. They stared at each other. Rosa could see a mound of dirt in front of the gate into the yard. Thirkel had gathered thin pieces of wood and was stacking them together, nailing them tight, building up the layers. He had made two solid planks: one long, one short. Rosa kicked her foot out, circling it around, a half-hearted ballerina, sending mini clouds of dust swirling. Thirkel picked up the two planks and nailed them together.

He lifted what he had made, Rosa looking on with interest, and jammed it into the mound of dirt.

She walked over to him. He was red in the face, puffing out his cheeks like a goldfish, droplets chasing themselves down his cheeks.

'Why have you put a cross there?' she said.

Only his eyes moved toward her. 'People are frit of crosses, keeps 'em away,' he said.

'Why?'

He shoved her then, on her right shoulder. She steadied herself with her right foot hard beneath her and was ready for it. He didn't like her asking 'why?'

'People are scared of dead things,' he said.

'I'm not.'

Thirkel looked at Rosa. He smiled. 'Well, you should be.'

'Dead spiders are better than live ones,' she said. 'They don't run over your fingers.'

He didn't answer. They both stood staring at the cross. The breeze blew gently in their ears, the sun rose overhead, the silence only broken by a bird calling from the tree by the latrine, 'Dee-daw, dee-daw.'

'What's that bird called?' Rosa asked.

Thirkel cocked his head in the direction of its call. 'It's a dee-daw.'

'Because of what it says?'

'What else?'

How useful, Rosa thought, not to have to ask any more questions of birds when they were named for their calls.

'Where's Bink?' she said.

'He's your dog,' Thirkel said. 'It's your business.'

When they sat opposite each other like this they were distorted mirrors in a fairground. He was a larger, crumpled version of her, though the eyes she saw were her own. She could see her own thoughts in them.

'He doesn't like to wander off,' she said, jabbing at the porridge she had made. It was dry and lumpy, but Thirkel still shovelled it in. He always ate what Rosa put in front of him, without complaint.

'We've all got to leave home one day,' he said, screwing his nose up as he tackled a congealed lump of oats.

Rosa turned her spoon around and scratched a word into the surface of the table.

Thirkel twisted his head to see what she had written. 'That's not how you spell it,' he said.

'What bit's wrong?'

'There's a u after the o and it's i, n, e at the end, not double-e, n.'

'Oh,' she said. 'Well, it's too late now.'

Thirkel shrugged and went back to his porridge. 'Suppose you'll be wanting one now,' he said, mouth full of food.

'One what?'

Thirkel tapped with his spoon at the word she had written.

'I don't even know what it is,' Rosa said. 'Someone said it on the radio.'

'It's a musical instrument,' Thirkel said. 'It rattles.'

'Oh,' Rosa said. 'No thanks.'

Tambourine, she thought. Tambourine, tambourine, tambourine.

An Eck-Eck called from her window ledge, but she refused to turn. Call all you like, she thought, I'm not listening. Her arms were beginning to ache but she fixed her gaze on a tree in the distance that bowed slightly toward her, in deference to her strength. The muscles in her upper arms started to shake.

'What are you doing?'

She had not heard her father's approach.

'You said people were frit of crosses.'

'I did,' Thirkel said. 'Who are you trying to frit?'

'Nobody,' Rosa said, holding her pose. 'I thought maybe Bink was frit and that's why he's run away. So I'm being a cross too, so he'll see me and know there's no reason to be scared.'

'Come inside, Rosa.'

'I don't want to.'

'You can't hold it any longer.'

She let her arms fall to her sides and for a moment they hurt more than when she'd had them raised.

'What's under there?' she said, looking at the mound of dirt beneath the cross.

'Nothing,' Thirkel said. 'Old tin cans, rusted metal, bits of junk.'

Rosa sighed.

'Come inside,' Thirkel said.

* * *

'You rely too much on that dog.'

Thirkel perched on the edge of her bed as if he were frightened it would tip up if he put too much weight down.

'Everything leaves in the end,' he said. 'You have to be ready.'

'Bink won't leave me,' she said.

Thirkel looked at her.

'And you won't leave me.'

The mattress pinged and groaned beneath them, adjusting to their movements.

'Who are you trying to frit with that cross?' Rosa said then. 'No one ever comes. Only Miss No-Name.'

Thirkel looked at her for a long time, but she could see that someone had switched off his eyes, so she said no more. After a while he stood and left the room.

'You just stay in here and keep quiet,' Thirkel said. 'I'll let you know when you can come out.'

'It's too dark,' she said, peering into the coal shed.

'It's the same place when it's lit up,' he said, hurrying her inside.

She supposed this to be true, but it didn't seem like the same place when the door closed behind her and the shadows closed in. She stood still and stared out in front of her. She could see a knot had worked loose in one of the wooden panels and she jabbed it with her finger until it popped out with a satisfying ping. The hole it had made let a pinprick of light through. She pressed her eye up to it, blinking at the colours that darted in. When her vision cleared again she could see her father, standing by the cross, his hand raised to his forehead, shielding his eyes from the sun. She wondered what he was looking at.

She pulled her eye away and looked at the pinprick of light on the floor of the coal shed.

If I had more of these, she thought, I would feel better.

She bent to her knees and picked the pinprick up, moving it to her left. Another replaced it, and she moved that one alongside the first, and so on, until she had gathered many lights and they shone in a semi-circle around her. She did feel better then.

She looked through the hole in the wall. Miss No-Name was talking to her father. She had not heard the car approach. Rosa had asked her name many times, but she said she would not tell her, and Thirkel didn't know it. She came two, three, four times a year. She would stand in the yard, talking to Rosa, until Thirkel noticed and came out, then she would get into her car and drive away. She never said anything interesting, just 'How have you been?' and 'What have you been up to?'

She was talking to Thirkel and she didn't seem at all frit of the cross... but yes... yes... she was. It was just that she had not seen it, distracted as she was by Thirkel, but he gestured down to it. Then she saw it all right. She screamed, just once, high and shrill, making Rosa jump, and sank to her knees, rocking back and forth.

Rosa watched, fascinated, feeling the warmth of the sunlight she had gathered, rubbing the back of her neck with its heat.

Miss No-Name stood and mouthed one word to Thirkel. He thrust out at her shoulder, pushing her away and nearly knocking her backward. *She* was not ready as *I* am, Rosa thought.

'You must never just ask why,' Thirkel always said. 'It annoys me.'

Rosa felt brave compared to Miss No-Name. *She* had not been frit of the cross. What a lot of grief, she thought, over some old bits of wood.

Her father led Miss No-Name into the house and Rosa watched the space where they had been for some time. Then she turned and sat down cross-legged on the floor, looking at the semi-circle of lights she had gathered.

When Thirkel let her out she did not know how long she had been sitting there. She thought she had heard Miss No-Name's car leaving, but she had stayed where she was. Thirkel led her out the coal shed, and the pinpricks of sunlight danced back out into the air.

'She won't come again,' Thirkel said. 'It's best that way. For you.'

'I didn't mind her,' Rosa said, though she really didn't care one way or the other.

Back in the house: 'Why have you tidied all my things away and left yours?' Rosa said. 'That's just silly.'

Thirkel shrugged.

Rosa wondered where Bink was. He had never gone away from her before. He had barely left the yard in the last few weeks, shuffling along, looking bored.

'You're all right here, you know,' Thirkel said. 'I do all right by you.'

'I know,' Rosa said. Then: 'I miss Bink.'

She kneeled down by the mound of dirt and rubbed her hands back and forth in it. The air smelled funny down here, earthy and fetid. She picked up a piece of wood her father had discarded and began to dig into the earth. Thirkel watched from the doorway. He made no move to stop her.

After a while she struck something and clawed at the earth with her fingers until she could get a grip on it. She pulled it out: a rusty old can. There was something else. A broken head of a garden fork.

It is just as my father said, she thought.

She replaced the can and the broken head of a garden fork and smoothed the earth flat with her hand. She looked at the mud trapped beneath her fingernails. When she stood she waved at her father. Thirkel waved back.

Her father was calling for her, and she did as he asked, though she did not hurry.

Thirkel stood in the yard and Bink was there. She stood still. Something was wrong with this picture. Bink dashed around her father's feet but Thirkel towered above him like a giant. She wondered if the light was affecting her eyes.

'He came back,' Thirkel said. 'Just like that. Unexpected.'

'That's not Bink,' Rosa said.

'Of course it is,' Thirkel said. 'Who else could it be?'

Rosa didn't know.

'He's too small,' she said.

'He's been away. He hasn't eaten for days,' her father said. 'He has wasted away.'

Bink, if it was Bink, looked healthier than ever before. He ran toward her and yelped, jumping up at her knees. He certainly looked like Bink. She wondered if he had always been this small and had only grown in her memory since he had been away. Rosa looked at her father. He looked as if he was ready to cry.

She gathered Bink into her arms.

'Where have you been?' she whispered.

She smiled at her father, and Thirkel smiled back.

'I shall make him a pen,' Thirkel said. 'For when he is out in the yard. We do not want him running away again. He is livelier than he was.'

'Shh,' Rosa said. 'He's sleeping.'

Bink had curled in her lap and closed his eyes. She rested her head on the back of the chair.

Thirkel went outside and after a while, as she started to doze, she heard the sounds of hammer and nail, hammer and nail. The swear word when it came she committed to memory. She would note it down later.

A pinprick of setting sunlight found its way through the blinds. Rosa reached up a hand and brushed it toward her face, letting its warmth rest against her cheek.

I have everything I want, she thought.

The sounds continued outside and then they stopped. She hovered on the edge of sleep. Thirkel came in and she felt him standing over her. He walked away, and then walked back. She felt a blanket being spread over her and Bink. Had she wanted to she could have opened her eyes, but she kept them tight shut and pretended to sleep, as her father fitted the blanket around her.

10
______

NEW HOUSE

WE ARE bemused by the appearance of a new house in our street. This makes it sound as if it grew overnight, which of course it did not. It appeared in a space we had not considered big enough for a house. Its newness made us all feel a little grubby by comparison and so we took against it. When cars pulled up and people got out to look around we took against them as well. We did not return their cheery waves; we crossed over to the other side of the street as we walked our dogs.

We gathered at coffee mornings, itching to discuss the appearance of this interloper, pleased for once not to be talking about whichever one of us had not managed to turn up that day, always wary then that word would get back to them of what we had said. It was not always easy to see where alliances lie.

Yet we were all united in our distrust of this new house.

'It is trying to be something it clearly is not.'

'I didn't think they were allowed to build there.'

'Surely it should be in keeping, nobody could say that *that* is in keeping.

New neighbours moved in and we studiously avoided them. We did not answer them when they knocked at our doors. In no time at all they gave up trying, with a casual indifference that offended us all the more.

But it was the reaction of the house itself that really got to us. When we looked at it, it lowered the blinds in its upper two windows as if it were closing its eyes against us. We knew full well the new owners had left for work and it could not be them. This was the house sending us a message. The roof of the porch seemed to tilt slightly so that it resembled an upturned nose; it said, 'I do not need you.' Birds began to alight only on the roof of this new house, snubbing our moss-covered tiles and singing their cheery songs.

We began to think we may have been hasty in our judgement. We queued, laden with gifts, cakes, biscuits, and our excuses ready.

'We wished to give you time to settle in.'

'I have been so busy. It is terribly remiss of me.'

'Goodness me, I am all over the place. I hadn't realised you had moved in.'

We jostled together in our eagerness to get to the front of the queue, and as we queued the house relented, raising its blinds a little to peer down at us gathered below, opening its mouth to let us in.

11

THESE ARE THE BEST DAYS

NICHOLAS WAS tired of his town. He was no longer a child and so people had ceased to be interested in him. Eyes at half-mast, he cast his gaze to the floor. He was the twisted coil of wire, the broken comb, the discarded fast food box, greasy and reeking, left strewn across the pavement. He was the rows of bleeding bin bags, ripped by ravenous foxes. Every drop of trodden chewing gum was a bully's push on a bruise. At school he travelled corridors scented by stale socks and exuberance to find the most out-of-the-way, undisturbed bathroom and contemplated his face. He was tired of being a boy. He had refused his six-week visit to the hairdressers and the ends of his hair were split, unkempt. They reached away from his head, pointing hair-clumped fingers in all directions. He tousled it about some more, tried the vacant and dejected stare he saw on his father's face each evening. Nicholas wished, now, to be a man. He thought about what he would do.

He went to the next village, a child of his own town, still holding on to its mother's hand, separated as it was by only a litter-strewn stream and a field the council had let become over-grown and untidy so it could be called a nature reserve. He went to the builder's yard, industrial and ugly on the edge of the village, and enquired if there was work to be had.

'When can you start?' the owner said, sunken eyes darting only once to Nicholas's face. It was the only question asked of him. There were papers strewn, multiple coffee cup rings like pie charts etched into spreadsheets, invoices, order forms. On the wall a calendar, two months behind, a bulldog leering out, a catchphrase that Nicholas could not read from across the owner's desk. He said he could be there in the morning. The owner nodded, placed a cigarette in his mouth, and Nicholas left.

He got up early the next day, an eyelid-crusting early that seeped into half-asleep skin and woke him more fully than he had been on any school day. At the yard he was paired with another worker and spent the day following jabbing points of fingers toward something to lift, something to carry, plaster and brick dust coating his clothes. Some of the other workers spoke little English, mumbled to each other and nodded in Nicholas's direction. When women came into the yard, which was rare, the workers whistled and hollered. There were rude gestures. Some of the women liked it, others clearly didn't. Nicholas half-laughed and semi-smiled (only when he was sure the women weren't looking), but didn't join in with the jeering.

The owner of the builder's yard was good natured. His stomach peered from his shirt, straining hirsute fingers against buttonholes. He clapped Nicholas on the back with nicotine-stained hands. He told elaborate jokes, punctuated by wheezing coughs, that Nicholas had trouble following, then began to laugh before he had reached the punch line. He bent double, sucking in breaths so he could get his words out.

'What has length to do with thickness?' he said when he had recovered himself, and the workers all laughed.

Nicholas was perplexed. He had lost the tenuous thread of this latest gag. 'I don't understand,' he said. This only seemed to make them laugh more.

———

The work was hard and the days seemed long. There was lots of heavy lifting, which pulled at his back and strained at his knees. He didn't mind. His days seemed to have a purpose to them. His brain felt more alive; it fizzed with an energy he had not found sitting behind a desk at school. His arm muscles grew stronger and more pronounced. His face and arms caught the sun and darkened.

He had told the school there had been a death in the family and he would not be in for a while. He had done a passable impression of his father on the phone that night, and again two weeks later, when the school rang.

'We didn't know Nicholas had a brother,' the school said in one of its many disinterested, disembodied voices.

'It was his half-brother,' Nicholas said in his father's voice. 'The family dynamic is messy. I don't need to explain myself to you.'

'No, no. Of course not.'

He received his pay in an inside-out plastic money bag at the end of each week. He bought cigarettes the first week. The taste was foul and he was not sure if he was doing it right. He practised on the way to the yard, but was wary of passing cars and sticky-beak passengers who may know his father. He bought a beer in the pub with the gang from the yard after work and was sick in the play area out the back, on his hands and knees, next to the swings, lurching back and forth in time with his stomach. The next time he had a Coke.

'My dad's an alcoholic,' he said when his colleagues poked fun. 'It's in the genes. No point encouraging it.'

A few had similar family tales, which they told in halting, accented English, and the evening took on a sombre tone. They stared at the pub carpet and its gaudy, dark, intricate swirls, designed for eyes and stains to get lost in. His choice of drink was not remarked on again.

If his father noticed the changes in him, he did not mention them. His father, who was not an alcoholic, had nevertheless always seen his son through a haze. If his arms were more defined, his pallor healthier, then it was to be expected. He was growing up.

Nicholas sliced a line in his mattress with a kitchen knife, pleased with the crisp pop as his knife dug in, and stuffed his earnings into the space. He had never got pocket money and so it seemed like a lot to him each week. He wondered if it was as much as it should be. He knew there were laws about that kind of thing, but after his attempts at cigarettes and beer he had little to spend it on. He kept the money in the plastic bags and liked the hollow sound of the plastic crumpling as he rolled over in bed.

As the months went by he found he was not as enthusiastic. The early starts pulled at his limbs and brain and there were days when he had to sideways dart down streets to avoid kids from his school. There were rainy days, but the work continued out in the yard and he came back home clammy and cold, his T-shirt sucking against his skin.

'Good day at school?' his father said.

'Oh, the best,' Nicholas said.

He began to wake in the morning with the same sense of resignation he had felt on school days. He struggled to reach the yard on time, breaking into half-hearted runs along dreary gum-spotted pavements to make up time.

There was no need, however, to feel this way. He had proved
he was in charge of his own narrow destiny. He went to the
owner of the building yard and handed in his resignation.

'It is time for me to move on,' he said. 'I am restless.'

'You are a young man,' the owner of the builder's yard said,
dipping his cigarette as he thumped Nicholas's shoulder. 'It is
hard to stay in one place, but you will learn the value of it in
time.' They parted with a handshake and Nicholas smelled the
nicotine on his hand when, stepping back out into the yard, he
wiped at his dripping nose.

A weight rose from his shoulders. He felt himself stand taller.
That weekend he helped his father with chores around the house
and ran several errands for a neighbour, eager for the week
ahead. He played garish computer games and listened to raucous
pop music, his speakers distorting with the bass-lines.

On Monday morning, he returned to school with a smile on his
face. He kicked discarded pizza boxes along the pavement until
crusts marked with molars and incisors skid out from the boxes
like rats. He was greeted warmly by his friends. They had heard
of his 'family problems' without knowing specifics, and he had
not told them where he had been. He avoided their questions,
steering the conversation instead on to the latest plastic fad toy
with minimal design and no purpose, and soon they were
running around the school as if he had never been away.

At his first lesson of the day though, he found he did not have
a seat, the first loser in a game of musical chairs he did not know
he was playing. His teacher faced him with a stern look and sent
him straight to the office. He tripped slightly as he left the room,
embarrassment grabbing at limbs, and there was a ripple of
subdued laughter, a breeze gathering desiccated leaves.

'We did not expect to see you back,' the school said, stern and solid as the bricks it was built with. 'It was thought you had left.'

'It has been a hard time for the family,' Nicholas said. 'But I am back now.'

His school trousers itched, electric fingers tugging at the hairs on his legs.

'Nicholas,' the school said. 'We know that you have been working on a builder's yard. A few of us have seen you in passing.'

He felt a shifting in his stomach, felt the porridge soaked with milk and orange juice, flecks of spit-swallowed toothpaste dotting the mass. He thought he may heave.

'It seems you are not as young as you have led us to believe,' the school said. 'There have been instances of it before, of course —grown men, reluctant to find their way in the world, claiming to be younger to stay in the school system. Reporters even, planting themselves to get a story for their editors. Whatever the case, Nicholas, there is no place for you here now.'

Nicholas was perplexed, this was unexpected.

'But I'm a boy,' he said, his voice breaking with a burping lurch and grasping at his younger self.

'Come now,' the school said. 'This is unseemly.'

Windows watched as he crossed the playground, lifting soiled sneakers over unlucky white lines. He returned home, his mind racing, and his father asked what had brought him back so soon.

'It is nothing,' he said. 'There is some trouble at school. I need my birth certificate. Do you have it?'

'Of course,' his father said. He went to get it, without asking the obvious questions.

Nicholas waited until he had gathered his thoughts. He traced his fingers over his mother's inked name, removed from his and separated from his father's. He looked at the word next to his own name. 'Boy.' He returned to school that afternoon with the slip of paper in his hand. He felt sure the misunderstanding could be dealt with.

'Documents can be forged,' the school said. 'It is easy enough these days, with the Internet and such like. Do not set foot on school premises again.'

Nicholas was not used to being challenged in this way. His head hurt, pressure digging at his temples, and he fought the urge to return home. He walked the streets, still clutching his birth certificate, unsure of where he was headed until he reached the gates of the builder's yard. He went in and found the owner.

'I don't know what I was thinking,' Nicholas said, placing his hands on the cluttered desk in front of him, finding chinks of desk space that were not quite in line so that his shoulders sloped. 'I don't want to leave here at all. I am taking back my letter of resignation. Let's pretend it never happened.'

The owner of the builder's yard had greeted him warmly, but as Nicholas talked a darkness spread across his face. Nicholas noticed he was not looking at him; his gaze was resting on the piece of paper that he still clutched in his hand.

'What is the meaning of this?' the owner of the builder's yard said, snatching at the paper. 'Is this true what it says here?'

Nicholas did not like being caught out; he could feel heat swelling his face. He thought for a moment.

'Documents can be forged,' he said. 'It is easy enough these days, with the Internet and such like.'

The owner of the builder's yard snorted. 'I can be reported,' he said. 'That is easy enough these days too, with the Internet and such like. Go home, boy.'

He spun the birth certificate back across the desk and shook his head.

Nicholas circled the village many times. He could not face the thought of being inside. He needed the air around him to counter the enclosed feeling he had in his mind. He walked the nature reserve, seeing none of the wildlife whose perky, colourful pictures brightened the boards erected here and there. Instead he saw garish crisp packets, ripped apart to show their flavoured insides, beer bottles arranged like a Stone Age circle, letting the sun hit the pile of cigarette butts in the centre. Tiny purple bags, swollen with dog shit, swung from branches: alien, unnatural sproutings. Soon, though, he felt the cold and trudged his way back to his home.

In his room, he stared at racing car wallpapered walls. The noise in his head fizzed and crackled. The wheels of the cars pulsed as he stared until he was sure they inched along the walls. Nicholas was a boy who liked to think things through. He went over all that had happened since he had decided to be a man. He began to see what he should do.

He put on his white shirt, blazer, and school tie, his itchy trousers and scuffed black sneakers, smoothed down his hair and returned to the school. He stood in the office in his school clothes, but when he spoke he spoke as if he was talking to the owner of the builder's yard.

He explained that there had been a mistake, that he had attended the school for many years. There were teachers in the school, he said, who had known him when he was little more than a baby. They could easily verify his story.

The school listened and nodded its head. It looked at Nicholas, with his hair smoothed down, his school clothes, and the earnest look on his face. It looked at the boys and girls running past its windows, screaming and hollering.

'I think you will be an asset to this school,' the school said. 'There has clearly been some kind of error, for which we can only apologise. I am sure we can locate the necessary documentation.'

He rejoined his classroom, his absences and office visits raising him to levels of interest he had never before reached.

After school he went home and changed into his builder's yard clothes. He tousled his hair about. When he got to the builder's yard and was spotted by his former colleagues he acted as if he was speaking to his friends at school. He shouted and yelled across the yard at them, his speech was littered with obscenities. The owner of the builder's yard leaned out the window of his cabin and beckoned Nicholas inside.

'I need this job,' Nicholas said. 'Just give it back, stop messing me about. That paper was nothing. I just use it to get teenage discounts at the cinema.' Then he swore. The owner of the builder's yard threw back his head and laughed.

'I was too hasty before,' he said. 'I knew there would be a rational explanation. Imagine you as a boy.' He sniggered and a bubble of snot popped from his nose, hastily retreating as a sodden sniff called it back in. 'The job is yours. We've missed having you around.'

'I can only work weekends though,' Nicholas told the owner of the builder's yard. 'You got me thinking, mistaking me for a boy. I am going back to school in the week.'

'What can you possibly learn there,' the owner of the builder's yard said, 'at your time of life?'

'Everything,' Nicholas said. 'I am as thick as two long planks.'

'Clearly,' the owner of the builder's yard said, throwing back his head with neck-crunching suddenness, and laughing. 'I think you mean as thick as two short planks.'

Nicholas looked at the owner of the builder's yard. 'What has length to do with thickness?' he said.

There was silence for a moment, and then they both laughed.

12

TINY INDENTATIONS

IT WAS ONLY to be expected she should want her own space. They were no longer children, after all, and were not joined at the hip.

Her mother had humoured her, setting an extra place at the table, a pillow and blanket on the floor by her bed. When these things stopped Harley did not seem to mind.

'He *is* there,' she had insisted. 'If he isn't, why are there footprints?'

'That is where the grass has grown in clumps,' her mother said, or, 'That is where worms have dislodged the soil beneath.'

There was always an answer, and it never involved Harley.

'Well, it is a shame you do not see him,' she said, exasperated. 'I can do no more to help you.'

'They could see you if you let them,' she said to him later.

'Parents can be blind to what is happening in front of them,' Harley said.

He held her then, in the way she did not like.

She had started bleeding. It was not a surprise. Her mother had prepared her; the school had explained things thoroughly. Still, it did not yet come naturally; she wanted her privacy respected. Harley, though, needed to be told twice and it tired her to do so.

'Can you not just listen to me the first time?' she said.

'I'm not used to your secrets,' he said, petulant.

'There's no secret. I just want some space.'

This was winter; it would take no effort to be cold. Her father had moved on, without, it seemed, a second thought for the rest of them.

'And I was here for you then,' Harley said, reading her thoughts, as he always did.

She tasted snowflakes on her tongue, nothing more than droplets of water. Harley stood by, in no mood to play.

The moment was expected, though she had not thought she would be the one pushing for it.

She held it back, until it was needed.

'You aren't real,' she said. 'Everyone told me. I should have listened.'

It was the worst thing she could say. They both knew it. He looked at her for the longest time, then turned and walked away. Her feet rooted to the spot; tears froze beneath her eyes.

When the snow finally stopped falling she could still see, stretching away from her, tiny indentations, each one pulling at her brutal heart.

13

SWEDISH MARBLES

IN THE YEARS before they studied me for research papers and medical journals I was left alone. But the gift my father gave me was too delicious to resist, the hook that grabbed the interest of the reader. Enquiries were made and my father accepted. I became an object of scrutiny. Had I been aware of my father's plans? they asked. I was aware of the noises of construction. Our house was often silent, it thrummed with it. Workmen came and fixed water pipes that creaked; light switches that hissed were replaced. Everything was done to keep the house quiet. The windows were triple glazed, so that it seemed we were looking at a picture of a window to the outside world. We were a little lost there, I think, the two of us. It could be stifling and calming in equal measure. I could close my eyes and imagine the world had disappeared, and this was not a bad feeling. On the TV once I had seen a film where a man had woken to find he was the only human left alive. It was not a film that scared me. Our silent cacophony hummed in my ears but I was acutely aware of any changes, so the noises at the rear of the house did not pass me by.

My room was at the front of the house. The upstairs corridor was wooden, with a strip of carpet running along it, so that it resembled a stately home open to public viewing; the carpet to protect the floor from the muddied feet of dawdling, curious tourists. There was wood panelling on the walls, and the furniture on the landing was old with many tiny drawers and doors, largely unused. The house did not feel as if it belonged to any of us; it let us know that it had been there long before us and would easily outlive us all. On the landing all rooms that backed onto the garden were locked. The last of these was my father's study.

Curious at the noise I approached his door. I held my knuckles up (I remember pausing to notice a spot forming in the hollow between two veins) and rapped on the door. I waited patiently as I had been taught, imagining, as I had been told, the time it would take my father to rise from his chair, straighten the line of his jacket, and progress his way across the carpet.

'Imagine me like this, and think how it makes me feel for you to knock again when I am halfway to you,' my father had said.

A key turned, the door opened a slither. My father slid out through the gap, closing the door behind him.

'Germain,' he said.

Father always greeted me in this way, with my own name, as if he needed reminding of it. There was a hint of a question too, as if I must always have a reason for wishing to see him. His glasses tipped down on his nose so that, when he peered down to look at me, it was as if he were choosing to frame behind glass the bags behind his eyes. They were the mottled grey of a winter sky; the muddy mixture I made with my watercolour set when using a light colour without sufficiently cleaning the brush. My father's tie was perfectly knotted; his collar pinched against his Adam's apple. I never saw my father in a state of undress until he was old and could no longer manage for himself, and then I saw how much he hated to be seen in that way.

'There are noises,' I said. 'They woke me.'

The grandfather clock in the hall below sounded the hour.

'We are having work done in the garden, trees lopped and chopped,' my father said. 'It is none of your concern.'

The only window on the landing faced the road to the front and my father was not going to budge. I knew not to push a point. I tipped my head, cartilage creaking, to peer beyond my father, though I knew he had closed the door behind him and there was nothing to see but the doorframe.

'Run along and play,' he said. 'Your tutor is away all week. You should enjoy the freedom.'

Mr Macklebury had travelled to Whitby to stay with an aged aunt and I pictured my tutor perched on a seafront bench eating a plain cheese sandwich with the crusts removed, while his aunt, whom he had not had the patience to wait for, clicked and clacked her way down the promenade—a combination of sticks and heels on stone disturbing his reverie as she approached.

My father smiled at me. It was a smile I saw often: a mechanical lifting of the lips that indicated our conversation was over. When I reached my bedroom door I turned to throw my father a cheery wave, but he had gone back inside his study and closed the door behind him.

My father's door remained closed all day. I sometimes stood outside and listened for sounds within, but could hear nothing. His study connected to the bathroom, which in turn connected to his bedroom so there was often no need for him to leave these rooms. Lily would take his food in and half an hour later come up to collect the tray. Though he could have been working, sleeping, or at his ablutions at any part of the day, I found when I listened that I imagined him standing at the other side of the door, eyes blank, shut down in some way until he would be startled by a knock at the door. I imagined he had no existence beyond the time he spent with me.

He was a travel writer and had given up his travels following my mother's accident, in order to look after me, he said. Though I had a tutor, and Lily and did not seem to benefit from his presence in the house. He continued to work, producing extended and revised versions of previous popular books which sold in similar numbers the second time around. When he had exhausted this avenue he pushed at his memories for new ways to approach a subject and so he passed the years of my childhood. When I left and he finally let my mother go he began to traipse the world again, but his writing had lost its edge—it was as if in his years of imagining he had conjured more from his memory than reality offered.

I read voraciously, seeking out books that were part of a series, never happier than when a set of books had numbers at the top of the spine and I could build a collection. My father allowed me one book at a time and I was allowed to write the title of the next one I wanted and hand it to him at breakfast. When I finished a book, Lily always had another title ready. Though, of course, it was my father providing these books, I was always absurdly grateful to Lily and would thank her profusely. I was a slow reader and liked to read books twice. If I didn't like a book or didn't expect to read it again, I was instructed to give it to Lily to take to a charity shop so 'another child can benefit, and it does not clutter up the place', but the hallway and landing and my father's study were lined with bookshelves filled with dusty old tomes of history and travel. Ponderous, heavy objects of Egyptian history and Greek myths that I would sneak looks at when I could, sliding the glass doors protecting the shelves, breath held, millimetres at a time so as not to make a sound. I delighted in these tales of pharaohs who married their own sisters and gods who changed into animals to entice their lovers.

My paternal grandfather, just before he died, carved me a replica of a famous viaduct though these arches increased in size from left to right and had brightly painted numbers above each arch. He bought me a bag of five marbles to roll at the arches and build a score according to which arch they rolled under. I began, then, to collect marbles, of all shapes and sizes, gathering them all in an old plastic ice cream container, which bent and buckled at the sides with the weight when I tried to lift it. I rolled them along the landing carpet, the best place with its long uninterrupted run. My maternal grandmother, who had been born in Sweden, gave me a bag of Swedish marbles. They were chalky, rough to the touch and chipped easily but became my favourites. They were exotic, these marbles from another country. I dreamed of foreign travel, flying in an aeroplane high in the skies, investigating the places my father had been, though I knew it was beyond me.

After my father had told me to amuse myself, I had spent much of the day in my room, reading. The noise had been distracting at first but as the day progressed it receded into the distance, though it was still there if I looked up from my book and listened hard enough. Lily brought my lunch to my room, and half an hour later collected the tray. She cuffed me half-heartedly across the shoulder and told me to clean my teeth and wet my hair down. I had nodded and smiled and done neither of these things. I tried to paint, but I had not improved in the past year and I was at an age where I was beginning to expect my creations to resemble what I was trying to draw. When they didn't I disappointed myself. I pulled the container of marbles from beneath my bed and took them out onto the landing.

The biggest glass marble (clear but for a dash of orange, like a goldfish swiped through the middle) rolled along the landing carpet and I tried to roll the others to hit it, careful to collect any marbles that rolled outside my father's door. It would not do for my father to slip and fall. The thought alone made me shudder, but there was nowhere else with enough space for me to play my game.

The percussive clicks of glass on glass would not be enough

to disturb him, but I took care to roll them gently so they did not leave the carpet, clatter onto the wooden floor, and knock into skirting boards.

But still it was hard to judge. One of the Swedish marbles rolled too fast, struck the goldfish marble on its side, setting off toward the stairs. My stomach clenched; my young years seemed often punctuated by this feeling so that I would often be doubled over in pain and Lily would have to bring me a hot-water bottle for my bloated stomach and some milky, flavoured liquid to quell the bubbling mess inside. I ran toward the stairway, reaching it as the marble teetered over the top tread, beginning its tap-tap-tapping way down the stairs. It was useless to try to catch it. It was already further down the stairway than I was willing to go.

I pressed my hands together, then, in the way children do and prayed for the marble to reach the wooden floor of the hallway, roll across it, and rest out of the way under the hat stand or bookcase, or between pairs of my father's shoes. Instead it teetered to a stop two steps from the bottom. Lily or my father would be climbing or descending the stairs at some point. I could not risk them treading on it. I could feel my head begin to pound and I pressed my hands against the sides of my face, squeezing the flesh of my cheeks to feel the skull beneath.

It is all right, I told myself, as I grabbed the stair rail. I do not have to go all the way to the bottom.

My heart beat erratically; two beats now and then where there should be one. I felt clammy. I wanted to cry out. I made my way down slowly. I knew that other children sat and bounced their way down the stairs, making a noise and listening to the way their voice box jumped, but I could not risk being so out of control. I reached the Swedish marble after what seemed like an age. Flecks of chalk had chipped off and I swept them up with the cuff of my shirt. I reached to pick the marble up, fearful my hand would shake and drop it in the middle of the hallway floor. I pushed it into my trouser pocket, feeling the cold touch of it through the fabric against my thigh.

In the room across the hallway I heard the apparatus keeping my mother alive, its tubes and machines wheezing like steam trains. I felt my own breathing settle into the patterns made by these machines. My mother had fallen from a wall she was sitting on, tipping backward as she laughed at something my father had said, and hitting her head. She had never regained consciousness.

'She didn't fall far enough, poor dear,' my grandmother said to me at the time. 'Had she been higher it would have all been over, quick and instant.'

'Had the wall been higher, she may not have sat on it,' my father said, but I was struck by this idea that my mother had not had far enough to fall. It took hold as thoughts often can in childish minds and I could think of nothing else.

I told no one of my thoughts, or what I had heard. I went upstairs that day and refused to come down. No amount of coaxing would convince me to leave the first floor. My father, in the end, snapped and dragged me forcefully down the stairs, out into the car, pushing me kicking and screaming into the doctor's surgery. I was calmed only by the fact that this doctor was two flights up.

My father talked about my mother's accident. There were tears, which surprised me. My father was not prone to displays of emotion, and if he had done any crying before about my mother's accident he had done it in private.

'He has always been a clingy child, wanting his mother to lift him up,' my father said. 'It is terrible what happened to his mother, but I can no longer humour him. He must stop this nonsense.'

The doctor suggested talking to me on his own. The room was large and the doctor's desk and the chair for me were situated in the middle of the room, so that I felt I was floundering in the middle of a swimming pool, desperately kicking my legs to stay afloat, unsure of my ability to reach the safety of the metal bar around the edge. But I reasoned the quickest way out of this room was to talk to this man, who looked down at me with concern in his eyes, who seemed to want to hear what I had to say.

'It has always been this way,' I said, once my father had left the room. I couldn't remember a time when my heart did not race at ground level. There were too many people, too many obstacles. To calm myself I looked to the sky, at tall trees, skyscrapers spaced out evenly against the horizon, imagining I was up there with them. I stepped up on low walls, stood on benches. Even on the ground floor of my own house I felt vulnerable, panic stricken, and this was the reason I always wished for my mother to lift me up. My mother's accident only highlighted these concerns, proving to me that I was right to be worried.

The doctor listened as I spilled out my feelings, nodding as I described how it felt to be on the ground.

'It is very strange,' the doctor said, inviting my father back into the room. 'Like nothing I have ever seen. He has, almost, the opposite of vertigo. He gets those same feelings when he is on the ground. We can try tablets for vertigo and see if the outcome is the same.'

There had been more kicking and screaming on the journey back. I caught my father in the eye with the toe of my shoe and the area around his pupils blackened over the following days. The tablets I took caught in my throat when I tried to swallow them, and the ache of them grazing my oesophagus was the only obvious result of taking them. My father lost his temper several times and tried to force me downstairs.

'You must see your mother,' he had screamed once, his voice higher than I thought it could go. 'How can you not want to see your mother?'

I did want to see my mother, very much. I wanted her to walk into my room and tickle me while I pretended to sleep, to laugh at my stupid jokes. I did not want to see her hooked up to machines. I stood alongside my father, whimpering and shaking, until he reached down, hauling me up onto his shoulders.

'Sorry, son,' he said as we left the room.

My father told me later that he had watched me inch my way back up the stairs after collecting the marble. He had wanted to tell me that I could fall a short distance and hit my head whatever level I was on, that danger was never where you feared it would be, but lurking behind the most innocuous objects: a brick wall, four feet high; a sunny day; a chocolate-chip ice cream; a careless, unplanned quip that makes your wife laugh and throw her head back. But he could see that telling me this would do no good, could in fact make things much worse.

'Children get ideas into their heads and nothing will shift them,' he said to me. 'I could see that you had taken against the ground, and that was that.'

I was concentrating on keeping my breathing regular, on walking quietly up the stairs without them creaking. My head was down and only at the top of the stairs did I notice my father's shining black shoes. I pulled back instinctively, fearful of further attempts to make me reach the ground.

'I have something to show you,' my father said. 'Come, you must not be so afraid.'

He took hold of my hand and led me through his study door. The curtains were drawn across the balcony window. My father nodded toward it.

'Go ahead.'

I had not noticed that the noises had stopped. I had been absorbed in my game and the thudding of my heart seemed much louder than the noises of construction had ever been. I could not imagine what my father had to show me. There was little I was allowed to touch in my father's study. I loved the feel of the curtains—thick, velvet, soft against my fingers. I reached for them and drew them back. Before me, a wooden walkway through the trees, stretching the length of the garden and further still. It was like the adventure playgrounds I had gone to with my mother. She had gamely hauled herself up ladders and slid, squeaking, down metal poles as she strove to keep up with me, joining in with my games of knights and maidens. She had stood on the highest ramparts and called for rescue and I had looked up to her and yelled, 'Do not worry, I'm coming.'

'It goes beyond our boundary, through the gardens of our nearest neighbours, across the road to your grandmother's house,' my father said. 'Planning permission was fraught, but I pulled a few strings.'

I looked at my father. I longed to explore, but I had noticed things about the construction.

'There are steps down,' I said, pointing toward them.

'You do not have to take them. But I thought it would do you good to have friends. Boys cannot resist climbing. They will come to you now.'

'But then they will only like me for this walkway.'

'It does not matter how they come to you. You are a normal boy, Germain, with an unusual fear. That is all. They will like you when they meet you.'

I was unsure, but I knew I would like to have friends. To gamely haul themselves up ladders and slide, squeaking, down metal poles as they strove to keep up with me, joining in with my games of knights and maidens. To stand on the highest ramparts and call for rescue so I could look up and yell, 'Do not worry, I'm coming.'

I stepped out onto the walkway, loving the way it creaked beneath me. I had not been outside for so long. Lily insisted on the windows in my room being opened, but it was not the same. Leaning against the wooden balustrades I took the Swedish marble from my pocket and held it over the edge. I can still feel now the rush of energy as I looked down, the pull I felt. I looked to my father. He nodded. I held the marble for endless moments, fearful of the result, blood rushing through my head, then dropped it and watched its descent. It hit the ground, shattering into several pieces.

I smiled at my father. I strode out across the walkway.

14

SUNFLOWER SEEDS

THE LIE when he told it was not a big one but it soured something between them, though she tried not to let it. She had made homemade soup and sent him to the shop for bread rolls.

'The ones with the seeds,' she said. 'The ones I like.'

His look said it all, and when he returned it was with plain white rolls, which were the ones he liked.

'It's not my fault,' he said. 'They'd sold out.'

Later, she had to go to the shop for something else and she found the shelves amply stocked with the rolls she'd wanted.

'What can I say,' he said when she confronted him. 'I just don't like them.'

'You should have just said. There was no need to lie.'

He sulked then, and there was an atmosphere between them.

Later, he felt the urge to atone in some way, though she could see he did not feel the weight of the transgression as she did. He went to the garden and came back with a plant pot full of soil. He took one of the rolls she had now bought and brushed the seeds from the top into the dirt, pressing them down with his thumb.

'There,' he said. 'We will grow sunflowers and you will always have seeds to dress your rolls.'

She tried to smile, but could not help looking down at the roll which, now shorn of its seeds, was indistinguishable from the ones he had first brought home.

'They won't grow,' she said. 'They will have been through some kind of process.'

She turned and left the room.

A week later and the plant pot still sat on the kitchen table where he had left it. She refused to clear it away. 'Let him move it,' she thought. She knew she had overreacted, that there was more to it than he knew, her conscience getting the better of her. She knew that she wanted things he did not yet want. They had discussed this at length. She liked to make him talk of it. It amused her to see him twist in discomfort.

'I will wait until you are ready,' she had told him.

She wondered how things sat with him, whether he gave it a second thought.

There were two green shoots poking through the soil.

'He has bought some proper seeds and planted them,' she thought, 'and he does not see that this is another lie.'

He smiled when he saw them and moved the pot to the kitchen windowsill. Perhaps this is a good sign, she thought.

She pushed the two stems together to bind them, feeling the need for them to touch as they grew. She placed her hands on her stomach, and felt the weight of the lie she had told him.

15

SHAKING THE HOLD

TEN YEARS into their marriage Jason and Gaudia hit a metaphorical bump in the road, a momentary mistake. Misjudged madness. It coloured something between them, for how could it not. For a while they toyed with the idea of going their separate ways, but they had a mortgage to pay, mutual friends, and enough residue of love, they felt, to build things back again. Jason started wearing skinny jeans, though he no longer had the thighs for it, and it was hard to pull them up, but it was a nod to the start of their relationship. Whenever Gaudia told the story of how they met she always mentioned the skinny jeans. Jason felt his testicles crush when he walked, in a way they had not done fifteen years earlier; he felt this was no more than he deserved. Gaudia, for her part, started wearing the darker shade of lipstick he liked, her lips a deep red rose. Its name was *Ethereal Vamp* and Gaudia wore a T-shirt with these words on it that she said was a free gift when she bought the lipstick.

But the one mistake coloured everything, so that when Gaudia smiled at something Jason said he felt she was smirking at his skinny jeans, and when Jason puckered his lips for a kiss,

Gaudia saw a mocking imitation of the way her own lips looked when smeared with *Ethereal Vamp*.

Jason, compelled more than Gaudia to talk about the mistake, thought they could avoid its effects if they put the effort in. Gaudia smiled thinly, which was not a look that went well with *Ethereal Vamp*, and said, 'Let's just move on. We need to put this in the past.'

When Jason went out alone, trudging the streets, tendons flaring, the mistake seemed to take on its physical form so that he heard a quiet set of footsteps feathering behind him. When he swung around she was, of course, nowhere to be seen. He tried to focus his mind on work matters: spreadsheets and deadlines, emails left unanswered, and when this failed him he counted from one to one hundred with beats of two between each number. It was one night, one mistake that he needed to forget. It did neither of them, he and Gaudia, any good to dwell.

But suppressing something that wished to rise to the surface was like pushing a balloon beneath water. The mistake was:

~ a gaudy, boisterous bird (making a nest in their house, it seemed)

~ a wispy taffeta curtain (when he and Gaudia sat in the lounge it hung between them, swinging in the breeze from the open double doors to the garden, obscuring their view of each other)

~ a moss-covered church roof gargoyle, perched on the banister, leering

~ every shadow in every room.

Jason knew he was becoming obsessed, blinkered. His mind was refusing to let go of one stupid night, and it threatened to destroy the peace that he and Gaudia were trying to cultivate between them.

They tried to make meals together, he and Gaudia, stepping by each other in the small kitchen without bumping elbows in the way only long-term couples can. They alternated their choices. Gaudia threw everything into a mean chilli con carne; Jason painstakingly built a lasagne as if it were an architectural project, then wishing to tear the whole thing down when the pasta sheets were chewy and the sauce insubstantial. The mistake was:

~ a two-sided mirror, reflecting their own images back at themselves, forcing them to see the look they each carried behind the eyes.

Sometimes, when they made the old, stupid jokes and laughed together, the mistake faded from their minds. They did not laugh together much anymore.

Jason wandered the house at night, creaking the floorboards. He perused downstairs cupboards and upstairs wardrobes; Gaudia could hear the squeak of the hinges. Jason listlessly meandered from room to room, making mental notes of jobs that needed doing, the lists becoming alternatives to the counting from one to one hundred as he went about his day. He lost focus in these tired stumbles and returned to the bedroom, only to stand by the bed, looking down at Gaudia, who feigned sleep as soon as she heard the bedroom door open. There were things he wished to say to her, things he wished to discuss. Apologies he wished to make.

It had only been one night. He remembered her perfectly, of course; he saw her in every detail exactly the way she was. He wanted these remembrances to be tainted somehow, to look one day and think, 'No, I have not got the hair quite right, there was more of a curl', or 'Perhaps her nose was not quite so long, the pores more visible', but he was sure he had it right and so he was unable to forget.

To shake free of her, Jason tried picturing inanimate objects that would focus his mind away:

~ hat stands

~ fridge freezers

~ full-length mirrors

~ bookcases.

Then when this did not work, he tried animals he would be happy to have skulking in the corner of his vision:

~ a golden retriever

~ an oversize rabbit

~ a jackass penguin

~ a hamster.

These things amused him momentarily, because what else could a jackass penguin in the workplace do, but his mistake was there, in all these things. Mocking him, aware he could not put it aside.

Jason and Gaudia walked along the Embankment, collars raised and woollen hats pulled low over their foreheads, fibres catching at stray eyebrow hairs. They had always walked this route when visiting London and there was a wealth of memories walking alongside them. Good memories. They knew they were risking these remembrances but thought it was worth the risk. To put some routine back in their life, some old, familiar routines. The mistake crouched on rain-sodden benches as they passed by; it was a sound that rang in their ears. Other walkers looked around and Jason and Gaudia stared grimly ahead as if nothing was happening.

When they returned home they kicked off muddy trainers in the hallway and Jason threw himself in the small velvet-backed chair that people only used at Christmas when the house was crowded. He nodded his head to his chest and pretended to be asleep, unable to bear the silence between them. Jason remembered bringing the chair back from Argos, along with other mismatched odds and ends when they had first furnished this flat and were clutching at items to fill a space. They had friends to help and Gaudia, waiting at home, said, 'Here come Jason and the Argonauts' when they returned.

Gaudia was motionless and the room was filled with sounds they didn't usually hear when they sat in it. There was a high-pitched whine from the electrical equipment in the corner, and the dust motes that sailed across the room seemed to fizz with energy.

They had decided to wait before starting a family and had had many conversations over the years about children, but one or the other of them was indifferent, or unwilling, or not yet ready and the conversation was shelved for another time. Jason wished now that there were children in the house, creating noise to break the tension between them, giving them less time to focus on a small mistake, a moment of madness.

'I don't even know her name,' Jason said, his voice thin with embarrassment.

Gaudia looked at him and rubbed at her eyes. She scowled. 'You keep saying that. Is that supposed to make any difference?' she said. She threw her keys at the velvet-backed chair, but they missed and clattered against the radiator behind, leaving a scratch in the paintwork.

'I can cover that up,' Jason said.

'Like you do most things,' Gaudia said.

Jason thought often of telling his friends, sharing the story over a third pint of lager, but the shame of it held him back, so that when they were all gathered together and he told a joke among them his mistake kept him from enjoying the ensuing laughter.

He knew that something was starting to loosen in his mind, that this was not at all healthy. It was one night. A mistake. Gaudia had tried to move on; he had to do the same.

Yet, it was the shame of it that did him in most of all. He knew he had friends who had done similar things, had caught tail ends of fights with their partners, heard the accusatory sniping, but his friends had smoothed things over or broken apart and started new relationships. They did not refer to these mistakes again, and so he seemed unable to bring it up and kept it to himself. He didn't think that Gaudia had told her family (was sure they would have said something to him if she had) and he certainly was not going to tell his. Gaudia was the only one he could talk to about it, but they had talked through it endlessly when it happened and she had asked that they not speak of it again.

But how were they to avoid it when it came with them every-where, as much a part of them as the extra weight they carried, the blemishes on the skin that had gathered over the years.

Jason and Gaudia went to the theatre; they took pictures on their phone of the safety curtain and tried to guess how much such an expanse of material had cost and how often it needed to be cleaned, but, when the curtain lifted, their mistake was there on the stage. There was a bed to stage right, and the actors were writhing around on it in a most unseemly fashion (completely inappropriate to the content of the play) so that Jason didn't know where to look. By the time they had finished the sheets were crumpled and strewn at the foot of the bed in complete disarray and Jason could feel the blush in his cheeks. Gaudia sat, stony faced, next to him and at the interval she asked to leave.

'I can't sit under a heavy floodlight, it is making me nervous'—the excuse a nod at his own propensity for glancing above him in theatres and cinemas to see if there were anything that might drop on his head. 'You can stay if you want,' she said, but it was clear that she didn't mean it.

'I'll come with you,' Jason said, 'but let's at least get an ice cream.'

Gaudia walked off then, teeth clenched to hold her words inside, and he skipped, like a scolded boy, to catch up with her. He thought how he had annoyed her and he thought how he had missed out on an ice cream, and both these things aggrieved him equally, which he supposed was part of the problem.

When they got home they sat at the kitchen table, opposite each other. It was their familiar way of sitting but it was odd without the food between them. They didn't catch each other's eye. Gaudia looked past him out into the garden, which was overgrown and ready for pruning. Jason noticed stains in the wood of the table, and scratches where a glass or knife and fork had knocked against it or been put down too hard.

'How often do you think about it?' he asked, his words barely audible. He was sick of being so pathetic, but he had no energy left to be anything else.

'It doesn't do any good to keep bringing this up', Gaudia said, unsure if Jason meant the actual act or the mistake as a whole. She had no wish to discuss the act itself any further than they already had.

'I think about it constantly,' he mumbles. 'I can't get past it.'

Gaudia looked surprised. When Jason was not with her she gave it little thought now. She stared down at her hands, clasped together on the kitchen table, and rotated her wedding ring.

'It's not helping me to talk about it,' she said. 'You shouldn't make me. We said we would leave it.'

Jason stared at her without speaking, leaving the space hanging in the air. He was aware the silence was asking too much of her.

Gaudia stood, her hands shaking, and the chair screamed her pain as it slid back on the floor.

'It doesn't matter how often I think about it,' she said, and walked away.

But over the next few days, when he had a distracted look on his face, Gaudia said, 'I am thinking about it now, but it is no more than a haze in the corner of my eye,' and Jason said, 'I have thought of little else all day,' and Gaudia nodded and they continued with what they were doing. Gaudia was always able to brush the mistake away as if it were an abstract, a burst of colour, a movement or sound, so that he wondered if the thought of it was doing Gaudia some bodily damage, some internal wrecking of the brain.

It was just one night. Jason lay awake in the early hours calculating the total number of nights he had spent with Gaudia, weighing them up against that one night—as fractions, as percentages, reducing the mistake down to its smallest part. But one night had a heaviness that tipped every set of scales.

He became consumed by the fact that he did not know her name, that he had not troubled himself to ask it at the time. If he knew her name he could write it on:

~ Christmas napkins

~ Manila envelopes

~ supermarket receipts

~ torn squares of wrapping paper.

Then fold them into paper aeroplanes and throw them away. Incinerate them.

He should have asked her name at the time, but he had not wanted it to be anything more than it was. It had not seemed important; he had other things on his mind. Things that seethed like snakes through his brain, smothering those cells that made his best decisions.

'Do you really think she is likely to tell you her name,' Gaudia said, a harassed sigh escaping when he brought it up again, 'if you find her and ask?'

'I just would feel better if I knew her name. She'd have a label then. I could think, "Oh, she's called Jane. I've known lots of people called Jane. She's just another person I've known called Jane."'

'But wouldn't every Jane you meet remind you? It would bring it all back instantly.'

He didn't agree. Jason thought of all the people he knew or had known called Jane. He had worked with a Jane once. She had had a weight problem, three children whose names all began with H (Harry, Heidi, and was it Hannah?), and sneezed when she smelled cigarette smoke. He had known Janes with:

~ gold rings through their noses

~ tattoos of Greek gods that covered their backs

~ unhealthy, outdated obsessions with Leo Sayer

~ a collection of garish flip-flops (two different Janes).

Yes. Jason thought that knowing she was called Jane would go a long way to shaking the hold she had over him. Gaudia did not agree. She could not stand his need to keep rehashing it over and over. It was like constantly poking at a bruise and wondering why it did not heal. She walked away from him again, wondering if this would, after all, be the thing that finished them off.

The one thing he wanted was the one thing he could not have. He was wrong to fixate on it. He could not track her down and ask her; that would be a terrible idea. He could not ask the image of her he had engraved in his mind; she had no more knowledge of her name than he did, being something that only existed based on his experience. The mistake had become such a part of his life now that he started to see it when he was:

~ dusting the sideboard

~ feeding the cat

~ taking out the recycling

~ reading the local newspaper

~ re-staining the skirting boards.

It had settled in so much it did the chores with him.

He was embarrassed by the hold this woman had on him, by

the fact he could not let her go. He worried what it did to Gaudia, to be constantly reminded. But he was not clinging on to her memory because he wished to remember her—he hoped that Gaudia understood that. It was something that happened to scores of relationships; theirs was not an unheard of situation. It was surely more common than those marriages that stayed untarnished by such things. But there was something stopping him from moving on. He should have asked her name.

Jason and Gaudia took a walk through the park and Jason felt the mistake as a thin, transparent gauze that wrapped itself around them. He leaned forward slightly to look into Gaudia's eyes, to see if she was thinking of it too, but her face was expressionless and she did not move her head to look at him. The silver birches they passed bent in the wind; he hoped the breeze was strong enough to whisk the gauze that surrounded them away. He held on to Gaudia's hand, but it felt as if they were walking through the park as the best of friends, rather than as husband and wife. Jason did not want it to torment him unnecessarily, but then he remembered how differently Gaudia experienced its effect to him, as abstract concepts, not as a real, flesh person who was involved, who was brought into their lives for the one night that changed all the nights that followed and went before.

'Are you thinking about it now?' Jason said.

'Not until you said.'

'What does it feel like?'

'A pain in my heart,' Gaudia said without turning her head.

'It's a myth that relationship pains can affect the heart,' Jason said, but he felt an answering pang in his own.

Gaudia stopped then and continued to stare straight ahead. She exhaled in a way that had finality about it. Jason stepped back slightly, as if to get a better view, though Gaudia had a look on her face that suggested he had brought up this subject one time too many.

'If you are going to keep talking about it,' Gaudia said, 'then there is no hope for us, don't you see? I don't want to keep hearing it. And this obsession with her name, it's not natural.'

Jason's eyes burned with the tears he was holding back.

'I just need to know her name,' he said.

Gaudia sighed.

She leaned over and whispered it to him.

16

ACROSS THE WAVES

SHE WROTE letters home to her mother, but something was missing. They both sensed it, across the waves, a lost connection. She hit upon an idea. She took a pair of scissors and cut a square from her favourite coat, the one she had had for so long. Her mother received this, unsure what to do. When the second piece arrived she understood.

Inside the next letter from her mother there was a pebble from her rockery. She loved her mother's tiny rockery, had always adored the way the pebbles framed the forest of bonsai trees that thrived in all weathers under her mother's care.

The letters crossed oceans; a pebble going one way, a square of cloth the other. The daughter arranged the pebbles on the mantelpiece. Across the waves her mother brought down her old dressmaker's mannequin from the loft. On it the coat was being remade, her daughter reassembled before her.

17

HOW EASY IT IS TO BREAK THINGS APART

AMMA NEARY'S father likes to make something beautiful and then break it apart. His quizzical eyes sit beneath a mess of red hair, giving him a wild look, so it seems that he takes pleasure in the breaking apart. Amma cannot stop the visceral pull at her heart when it happens.

'You can't do this,' she cries, each time it seems, her hands up to her mouth, though it is her eyes she needs to cover. 'How can you bear to do this, Papa?'

John Neary laughs, because what else is there to do? Irritation patches through his veins—he feels it bubbling, around his heart, at the side of his head. He pats her twisting black hair down with calloused hands.

'It is my job, child,' he says.

He has tried to gift his daughter one of his creations, boxed and fancily bowed, but Amma will never accept them. She would rather have the thing whole, before he has taken his blades to it.

When John Neary's flattened Fenland town was small, people were content with small things. He was famed, then, for his puzzles. Animals, birds, rural scenes, anything that was wanted, finely carved in wood then cut into pieces. Large pieces for children; smaller, intricate shapes for adults.

The blades churn, decibels rise. It is dangerous work. The concentration knits his face like cosmetic surgery. He prides himself on having never cut himself.

'Though when I do, I suppose I will lose a finger,' he says, holding the back of one hand to her with one digit bent forward. 'The first time will probably be enough to set me back.'

Amma stands in the doorway of the shop, watching, always hovering on the threshold, ready to run if it overwhelms her. She hangs on the doorframe like she did as a child, thinking this must be the way to his heart; this will stop the blades gouging into the work he has created.

The varnish on the door is flaking and the wood is exposed beneath. There are scratches on the lock where they scrape their key around, trying to find the hole. These are things that once her father would not have left on show, but Amma knows he does not sell as many puzzles as he once did. She feels the wood give a little and lets go in a hurry so that when he looks up she is unsteady on her feet.

The new department store at the edge of the town sells games of all kinds, and there is no waiting list to be added to; you can simply stride in and buy them.

'Where is the fun in that?' Amma always says. 'Where's the an...ti...ci...pation?' stringing this last word out so it represents what it describes.

Now new estates are built on the outskirts and the commuters and young couples who move there seem faintly embarrassed to gatecrash the original town. They wish to edge outward to stock their cupboards, buy their toilet tissue, pay their lottery money. As shops open around the edges, the opposite happens in the heart of the town: boards go up, windows smeared and misted with white paint. John Neary has only ever slaved away in this insect-bitten, creaking shed at the back of their house, with a door from their garden, and an entrance open to the street that runs behind their house so that when both doors are open paperwork soars in whichever direction the wind takes it and Amma is sent scurrying after it. He has never aspired to anything more than this. He wished only to make his puzzles and put food on their table.

Her father screws up his eyes. He does this while he pictures where the cuts will go. When the blade starts its back alley jabbing motion, she sees it elongate in her mind and reach into his eye. She sees it shudder loose from whatever holds it in place and launch itself up to embed in her father's forehead. She feels an overwhelming desire to distract him.

She holds up two marbles, with swishing patterns inside, one to each eye.

'This is my crazy look,' she says, hollering above the din, and her father smiles.

'When will you be using that?'

'I'm practising for when I am old. I shall be able to jump to the front of the queue in shops, like Mad Virginia.'

There is a speeding up of ageing as the skin falls on John Neary's face.

'You should not speak of her that way. I expect more from you.'

Amma is indignant. He has misunderstood, that is all. 'No, there is a shop called Mad Virginia. It just opened on the Templeton estate. They named it after Virginia Pinner. They said then she has good reason to jump the queues.'

'I never know when you are toying with me, Amma.'

Her name backward the same as forward, so in a way she feels she is going nowhere.

'I don't know what you mean,' she says, twirling the marbles in front of her eyes.

Amma does not like to be set against her father in any way. She wishes to understand, but also she can see other ways of doing things.

At the bottom of their garden there is a tree. A *Quercus robur*— this is how she thinks of it. Her mother told her the name, told her it was a special thing that most girls wouldn't know. Her mother had died four years ago, from 'a blot on the heart' they said when asked. A tiny sentence for the agony she went through. But her father said that Mabel Neary's life was bigger than her loss, so they narrowed down her end to its smallest component so it would not come to define her.

Amma blocks out the blade's rattle and searches among the branches that drape her shoulders. She plucks the biggest, most beautiful leaves she can find. In her room she opens her fitted wardrobe and sits on the floor. Her father seems not to know she does this. When he looks for her he shouts at the stairs, giving her time to emerge, or pokes his head around the door and assumes she is elsewhere, allowing her to follow behind and wait to say 'here I am', so that he gives her his quizzical look as if she has done something he does not quite understand. Amma cuts the leaves into pieces with scissors and spreads them out on the floor in front of her. She has bought glue with her own pocket money. The edges of the leaves are too fine to seal together so she layers them on top of each other to get them to fix.

When the glue has dried she takes the scissors and snips around where there has been an overlap. Amma looks at what she has created. Irritation speeds her blood. They are not the same as they were. The leaves are back in the shapes they had before, but the lines where she has cut are visible and she feels they are ruined. She screws up what she has done, pulping it in her hand so they bleed their insides and stain her fingers. She throws the congealing mess in the bin. At the window she sits, staring out at the tree, apologising to it for the waste. She has heard that trees are connected beneath the ground, that they can warn each other of dangers from insects, can arm themselves. She does not wish it to turn against her.

Patches of light shaft toward her between the leaves, beams that are cut off each time the wind moves, then return again as the tree sways back the way it has come. The light warms her face. Amma looks at all the leaves and imagines them all cut into pieces and reassembled, the joins visible throughout.

She visits her grandmother. When she has a problem that needs solving this is where she goes. Her grandmother is a wise woman.

'I am not wise,' Jezra Peckleton says whenever Amma refers to her this way. 'I am old. When you live long enough people think you know a thing or two.' She sucks her lips in around her gums. 'Which I suppose is true.'

Amma tells her grandmother of her compulsion to glue her father's puzzles back together, of her experiments with the leaves.

Jezra is amused, has always looked fondly upon this child.

'One day you will feel pulled apart,' she says. 'By life, by a man. By your child turning their back on you. By hurtful things said and done to you. When you put yourself together again it's possible to still be what you once were, even if the joins are visible.'

She has said the wrong thing—she sees how Amma's face falls. She is a grandmother to this child only moments here and there in a week; she thinks that Amma does not consider who she is outside of this time. But this is not true. Once Jezra had a fall and was sent to the county hospital to recover. There Amma and her father timed their visit at the same time as that of a neighbour of Jezra's and Amma did not recognise her grandmother and the easy way she laughed and spoke with this friend.

'Equally,' Jezra says, backtracking, 'if you work at it enough, you can be torn in two, repaired, and there be no sign of what has occurred.'

Amma nods and tries to understand, her brain whirring loud enough for her to hear it rushing in her ears—this is the sound John Neary's blades make as they spin into action.

'Your father is happy,' her grandmother says. 'Do not cause discord in your last days together.'

Jezra has said something she shouldn't.

'It is best you talk to your father,' she says.

———

Clods of rain are falling—perhaps this rain was falling before. Amma had not noticed then; now, each drop of rain is a cold slap from her father as she hurries home.

She is shouting before she has even got through the door. Her father listens, caught out in something he had wished to tell her himself, but he had not been able to find the words.

She is to be sent away to a distant uncle, a man who when she conjures his image has no more reality for her than a character from a book she has read. She is to work on his farm.

'I know nothing of farms,' she says to her father, imagining all sorts. 'I do not understand.'

'We have need of the income,' he says. '*I* have need of the income. It is only as others do.'

She knows it is useless, knows also that he will only stand her anger for so long. He only tolerates it because he has been afraid to tell her and she has found out. She dashes to the door, as eager now to put distance between them as moments before she had been to close it; she runs back into the street. She slows to a miserable walk and ponders a future she has not planned for herself.

Amma is walking where she is not meant to walk. The industrial units are clamoured together, brazen in their corrugated ugliness. But she is not alone in her edging away from others. Virginia Pinner is crumpled by the kerbside, crying. She is wearing the coat she has always worn and has, beside her, the trolley she always wheels through the village. Children call her Virginia Pisser. They say she pisses herself, though she has only done this once as far as anyone remembers. It was the fact that she was unconcerned by it that has lodging in people's minds. She was at the bus stop and let out a mild 'ooh' of surprise as the piss wet her stockings and pooled around her feet.

She looks dishevelled. Hair asunder, Mabel Neary would have said, though she always had a kind word for her. Then again her father's hair has a mind of its own, so perhaps she saw something of him in this woman. An ornament she has bought from Mad Virginia's has knocked against something else in her bag and broken into three pieces.

'It is ruined, it is ruined,' she screams. 'I do not want it. Nothing can be done.'

Amma sees the simplicity of the child in this adult, sees that this is not something she herself will be able to hold on to, this feeling of childish emotions. She sees that there are more adult ways to approach things.

Amma takes the pieces of the broken ornament in her hand. It is a ceramic giraffe. The breaks are clean, at the neck, and two of the legs. She takes the tube of glue, still in her pocket from when she worked with the leaves, and squeezes the adhesive thinly along the broken edges. She holds the pieces tightly together, shifting them until the joins can no longer be seen. Virginia watches her.

'Don't you mind?' Amma says, nodding at the logo on the woman's bag. 'The name of the shop, I mean.'

Virginia rubs at her tears, smearing them across her already dirty face. 'I don't mind it.'

'My father thinks it's disrespectful,' Amma says.

Virginia shrugs. 'He's just jealous. I'm like him, with a shop named for me.' She looks at Amma. 'That's all anyone wants, isn't it?' she says. 'To get their name out there, get them all talking.'

They sit quietly then, waiting for the glue to dry, and when it is Virginia squeals and hugs Amma so tight she thinks she too will break.

'You have worked a miracle,' Virginia says. 'It is like new.'

There is a vein, or blood vessel, that stands out from her father's forehead when he is angry. She has made it appear. She will not leave, she says, over and again. He cannot make her. He can and he will, he says.

They dance around the room, him ready to lash out, her staying just out of reach. She is angry with her father; she thinks she has every right, and says something she shouldn't about her mother being dead and him being alive.

The flour mill ornament. A gift from her mother to her father when they first met. He had worked at a flour mill when he was still a boy. He had told his future wife how much he missed it. How exciting it had been. She had given him the ornament the following week. Now it is in pieces at Amma's feet; the mill wheel has come apart completely, has rolled between them. Her father does not like this loss of control. He leaves the room and she begins to gather the broken pieces as she always does. Before, she would place them in a bag and push it down to the bottom of the bin so he would not be reminded.

It is not easy. A small piece has chipped and she does not have it. She goes back to the room, hoping her father has not returned, and crawls around on hands and knees until she finds it, catching it with her fingers as she brushes back and forth, so small she has not seen it though she is looking directly at it. She hates the way the carpet tickles against her fingers, imagines the abrasion altering her fingerprints. If I commit a crime, she thinks, I shall rub my fingers here. She places the fleck of china onto the tip of her finger and walks carefully back to her room.

In the morning she makes a tray of breakfast things for her father and leaves it outside his bedroom door, knocking once. This is how she fixes things between them. Now she has something else to offer. She places the ornament in the centre of the tray. The tray is a garish red and in large white letters says 'Keep Calm and Keep Creating'—a gift from a customer. Amma has turned the ornament in her fingers. There is a slight crack still showing on the base, but otherwise she is pleased with her work.

She is sent to her grandmother's on an errand, her father's face a statue-set version of itself, and she thinks she has miscalculated, but when she returns her father stands outside the shop, a stupid grin on his face and a tuft of red hair pointing at what he is so pleased about.

He has altered the sign above the door. It now reads: 'John Neary & Daughter: Wooden Puzzles & Restorations'.

The sign is crude, no more than a scrap piece of wood nailed over the original 'John Neary's' sign, with new letters in white paint, a solitary drip cruising down from the tail of the 'g', but none of that matters. It is the words themselves that hold her attention.

She runs to her father then, and he holds her tight. She

knows he is embarrassed by what occurred between them, but knows also that she has impressed him.

'People will pay to have repairs done here when they see what you can do,' he says, looking her in the eye. 'Such fine work. A farm is no place for you. You will stay here, with me.'

<hr>

She holds the argument in her mind, in minute detail. She sees what she has done. Her father has a volatile temper; he throws things. She had manoeuvred him around the room, delivering her blows, saving the last for the moment he stood beside the ornament. She had not expected it to work; this is what she tells herself. This is how she settles the thing inside her. She looks to her father, then up to the sign, and offers a silent prayer of forgiveness to her mother.

A flake of paint is coming loose from the woodwork at the front of the shop. She pulls at it absentmindedly as they go back inside.

'Always trying to fix what is broken,' her father says.

18

——————

THEN

IT HAD BEEN SUCH a little thing.

She had made a noise in the back of her throat. Somewhere between a gurgle and a belch, he wasn't sure. She turned to him and smiled. That is when he knew. She wasn't the girl for him.

But they had that wedding to go to in three weeks. Her cousin, removed in some way—once or twice. She'd worn a red gown that day that had moved a split second after she did, like there was a shadow following her. He had said nothing.

Then she had suggested an American road trip and the idea had appealed, so he had agreed. They had laughed, their personalities grown as big as the tall buildings that brushed the sky, and nothing had seemed too hard to bear.

Then there had been the girl in the bakery, with one eye larger than the other, which she played to comedic effect. No one could raise an eyebrow quite like she could. That had been the moment, the moment. And he had tried to tell her one night, but she had shushed him, placing a finger on his lips and with her other hand taking his and placing it on the flat of her stomach.

That was that. A door creaked shut somewhere and latched. The flat stomach grew, and for many years that was that.

Then, when the children had grown, had silenced the house again as they left to make their way in the world, he had let those thoughts into his mind again.

Then her mother had sickened, and he had felt sickened by the commodes, the soiled bed sheets, and the sickroom stink that pervaded every inch of the upper floor. Then when her mother passed he had comforted her, and she had taken a long while to recover.

Then he had seen his face staring back at him in the mirror one morning and been taken aback by the unkindness of accumulated years. Then he had known for sure that he had left it too late.

Then he had resented her for taking away all the right times when he could have told her, all the times he could recall and all the ones he had forgotten. He had not been nice to her in her last years.

Then she, like her mother, had sickened. He had to deal with the commodes, the soiled bed sheets, and the sickroom stink that pervaded every inch of the upper floor. He had marvelled then at what she had done for her mother.

He had held her hand as she had shuddered with fear. He had talked to her of their American road trip, of the red dress she wore to her cousin's (once or twice removed) wedding. He realised that she thought he had always loved her. Then she had passed.

And then... then... then he wished he had always loved her.

19

____

THIS BELONGS TO JOY

THE CHILD HAS WANDERED; it is not a rare occurrence. Children wish to explore, to insinuate themselves into small spaces. Somehow Beatrice has found her way to the morgue. She has seen a body laid out on the slab. It has been explained to her but this has made things much worse.

'Do not let that happen to me,' she tells Joy. 'I do not wish to end up there.'

Joy looks at the child, at the fear in her eyes. The plea strikes at her; when she nods she knows what she is agreeing to, she knows it is not a promise she can honour.

She knows, too, that it will haunt her if she fails this child.

Beatrice doesn't wear a scarf like the others do and she is applauded for her defiance, her bravery, but Joy can see in her eyes that she is already defeated.

⸻

When Joy wears the right shoes she can walk these corridors and not make a sound. It offends her ears when trainers squeal, when high heels clop like tiny horses. Beatrice is in bare feet and they drift along together, a silent haunting.

In these corridors there is a hush, a reverential silence. Even when there is laughter, chatter, it is there at the ceiling like risen heat. Joy is sensitive to the sounds nearest her: the swish of a blind as they pass; a fly bouncing at the window, unsure of why its path is blocked. She is drawn by the greenery of the courtyard gardens. There has been a push from the hospital in recent years to improve its courtyard spaces, make them havens for staff and patients alike.

Still, there are broken chairs, tables, hospital gurneys stacked there, amongst the cigarette butts. But each plant, each tree, gamely reaching for the sun as it passes over the high hospital walls, each one catches her eye as she passes and gives breath to her lungs, gives the strength she needs to trudge these stark corridors.

There is artwork on the walls too, but she has learned not to be distracted. In her first weeks there she would stop and study the ones that caught her eye as if she were browsing a museum gallery. Her line manager swung silently into place beside her.

'They are for the patients, not the staff. We must be blind to them.'

Her name is Joy. The name badge is an affront to some people. She has had comments. 'It is not my fault,' she used to say. 'Blame my mother.' When situations are tense she finds herself covering the badge with her arm, but often the family look for it to thank her by name and she can see the slight flinch, that this is not the time for Joy.

Joy takes Beatrice to the chapel. It is old and ornate, yet still it is at threat of demolition to make way for a multi-storey car park. It doesn't look like Beatrice needs to know this.

In each day there are pockets of silence, some sense of an exchange being made. For every birth, a death. Joy and Beatrice sit alongside each other and stare ahead at the altar. The sun hits it through the windows, and when clouds cross the sun and the brightness dims, the altar looks as if it is falling.

'I love your name,' Beatrice says.

'Let's get you back to the ward.'

There is a party at lunch for someone who is leaving and she has made a banana cake. She began baking later than she wanted and her eyes were drooping as she finished. The girl in the flat below watched episodes of *Game of Thrones* back to back and Joy tried to identify scenes of sex and violence from the muffled shouts and cries that shuddered through the walls. 'Sex,' she said aloud, or 'Violence.' She caught her reflection in the window as she said 'sex', a sheepish grin on her face, and poured herself another cup of tea.

The work ethic here is distributed unevenly. There are some who charge at the work with a passion; others, at Joy's level, seem to see the day as some sort of social gathering, wandering from corridor to corridor to catch up on the latest celebrity gossip, television, music. They balance folders under their arms as if this shows they are hard at work. The party fizzles out because for some this is no different than the rest of their day. Joy does not engage with this gossip, and not only because it holds no interest for her, but because she believes in the work. She is given things to do and she does them, because why would these tasks be given if they were not needed? It is a simplistic view of the world and it has served her well.

When she walks back to her ward Aaron is there, standing at her desk. He is running his hands over the collar of her coat and she can see the name tag there. Her coat has her name inside because things go missing here. He asks her how she is and she says 'fine' because there is nothing to tell. He always has the look about him of someone who has just rifled through her things, though there is nothing here that is really hers, or that she would mind him looking at.

He took her to a hotel the first time, as if this promised something. The curtains didn't match the carpets and when she said this she remembered sniggering at the saying in her schooldays.

All the people she laughed at have done better than her it seems, as if this is a righting of a wrong.

They have not left the hospital for other encounters. She has bent forward on his desk; pressed herself in the stationery cupboard, noticing, at the back, green treasury tags that she didn't think anyone used anymore.

'We have an arrangement,' Aaron said, after the first few times, 'that suits us both.' She finds herself wishing him relocated to another hospital. These things happen, doctors and consultants moving around. She thinks she will be better without him, but the baser parts of her think of him late at night and when she wakes in the morning she is disappointed in herself.

When he asked for her help in a conspiratorial whisper she knew then that it had been his intention all along, but she felt content to have an explanation at last. There were papers, he said, that he needed to be rid of. She shouldn't ask any questions, she wouldn't understand anyway, but they needed to be disposed of away from hospital premises. He gave her slim folders at first, which drew no comment as she walked along the corridors and out to her car.

'I would prefer burning them,' he said.

She drove out into the country, bumping down uneven tracks. She read some of the pages, but found nothing there to interest her. There were unforeseen side effects, the word negligence cropped up. The subterfuge seemed foolish. In her daily work she made copies of everything, despite the hospital talking about going paperless. Whatever he tried to destroy, there would be another copy, somewhere.

If she is confronted she will say she thought he was joking, being overly dramatic to gain a laugh, that she had shredded everything on hospital premises and thought nothing of it. If she denies the other stuff they will look her up and down and believe her over him.

The first pages he had her burn she simply held in her hand and touched a lit match to them. The black flakes rose into the air like the opposite of confetti. But soon the folders grew fuller.

The incinerator she bought quite cheaply from a DIY store. The fires burn harder—there is nothing left but ash. She comes back a day or so later and scatters them across the fields.

She likes to unbutton his shirt, stand behind him and put her hands over his heart. When things start up like this she is removed from herself in a way she likes. They have to muffle the sounds they make. It is like doing it with the sound turned down; it is like not doing it at all.

He touches his little finger to hers sometimes as they pass in a corridor and she knows he expects her to feel a jolt of electricity, but she feels no more than the tickle of a money spider crossing her skin, though she knows this feathering of her cells will not bring good luck.

She has always been swayed by the directions of others, seeming to have no mind of her own when with anyone else. She does not know why this is. It is why she prefers to be alone.

'How do you work in that place?' her mother says, as if good things do not happen here, lives saved, new life arriving.

She finds time to visit Beatrice. She reads to her, and they talk as if there is no age difference between them. Joy finds that something in the way she acts or speaks can make Beatrice dissolve into laughter, and she finds that she, too, is able to laugh.

She remembers her father's joke, oft repeated, that her mother had 'brought Joy to the world'.

Though it is not spoken of again, there is a silent acknowledgement that passes between them of the promise made. Joy meets Beatrice's mother and finds she cannot look her in the eye, though it is clear her mother sees Joy as just another member of the hospital staff and nods only briefly her way.

Joy talks to the nurses on duty and they clench their lips together and shake their heads. 'Not long now,' they say. 'She is up a lot in the night, being sick. She is unable to pass water. The mother wants her at home, but it is too much for them. We keep it light in front of her,' they say. 'There is no need for her to know.'

She's eight, Joy thinks. She is not stupid.

***

'This is getting silly,' she says to Aaron. 'Just give me everything you wish to dispose of. It will be easier that way, for both of us. It will all be over and done with.'

It is the most she has ever said to him in one go.

He has a key to the security rooms and knows when they are

unmanned. He turns the cameras off in the three corridors she will walk down and at the back entrance where she pulls her car up. She asks him to turn off two more and he squints at her, but nods.

She takes a hospital gurney and waits until everything is ready.

It is hard to manoeuvre everything into the boot and her whole body tightens with the fear she will be discovered. She is grateful when she can turn the key in the ignition and move away.

She parks the car at the end of the uneven track and struggles to unload all she has in the boot. She fills the incinerator, stuffing files down the sides to plug all the gaps.

She tries not to think too much about what she is doing. She strikes a match and pushes it in the holes at the base of the incinerator and watches the flames catch, the fire escaping up a sheet of paper as if it has been caged too long, as if it knows what it must do.

She runs, not wishing to catch even the barest whiff of what this may smell like. She is fearful that when she turns the flames will have guttered out but they are raging, reaching their fingers to the sky from the holes beneath the incinerator's lid; they point the way heavenward.

She feels a surge in her stomach as if she is about to be sick and runs back to the fire.

Lifting the lid with a stick she takes off her coat, rolls it carelessly into a ball and throws it in, sees the name tag catch and burn as she lifts the lid back into place. In one of the hospital corridors she has noticed a smudge on the wall. When she got closer she realised it was a signature. Stepping back it was as if an artist had signed his name to the blankness of the wall, of the corridor, of the very hospital. She was moved by the thought of someone signing this wall, and different scenarios of why this should be have scrolled through her mind since. Passing that way again she could not find the signature, or it had been removed... or she had dreamed it—she is unsure which. That is why she threw the coat. She wants something of herself in there, burning; something to say that she did this.

———

It begins to rain, no more than a light drizzle. She feels the ebb and flow of it, counts every drop that falls on her sorry head. Her mind wanders until she loses sight of why she is there. She stares, eyes glazed over, ahead of her, at the way the scene above the incinerator shimmers in the risen heat. When hours have passed, and it is dark, she takes a torch, lifts the lid and uses the stick to prod at the embers, pushing them around, bringing them back to life, then scattering them apart so they die down again.

She does not know if she can go back, but she supposes she will. She will walk into work tomorrow and distance herself from the storm that will brew in a little corner of the hospital and then spread. She will march up to Aaron and tell him if he wishes things to burn he should be prepared to strike a match. She will sit down at her desk and begin the work that has been left there for her. She will buy another coat and sow another name tag.

20

———————

LITTLE WHITE LIES

SHE GREW THEM IN A POT, her little white lies, plucking them out to give to her husband before they got too big and darkened. I am just going to the shops, she said, I will be as quick as I can, handing him another white lie and later sipping coffee in the supermarket café, a full trolley of shopping beside her. He does not understand that I need time alone, she thought. I am doing no harm.

I have joined an aerobics class, she said. I am not getting any younger. Her husband did not comment, so she felt no shame as she drove fifteen miles to another village and sat in the public house.

He is always muttering about something or other that I have done wrong, she thought as she sat there, trying to look inconspicuous. It is only his way, I know, but it does not mean that I wish to hear it.

———————

The lies did not need much attention; it did not seem to hinder them whether they were in daylight or shade. Her husband took them when she offered them without comment. He had always left the gardening to her.

She took her car in for its inspection and it passed with flying colours.

It needed a lot doing, she said to her husband. I knew it would. There have been rattles and unexplained noises.

He counted out the notes from his wallet and later she counted them out in the dress shop. He would want me to look my best, she thought, out in public as I am.

The lies were longer than she remembered and starting to darken at the tip. They were not in any gardening books she was aware of so she was unsure how they should look. They are still mostly white, she thought, and can hardly be called anything other than small.

I have made a new friend, she said. Her name is Lesley. And she thought of the man who had smiled at her across the room, who was not called Lesley. Her husband nodded without looking her way.

He is comfortable with me as I am, she thought then. It would be wrong of me to trouble him in any way. I would not wish to hurt him. I could not hurt him if I tried, she thought, since I have done nothing wrong. She passed him another pot and readied herself to meet her friend who was not called Lesley.

Her husband held on to her lie. He studied the pot. Untended in recent days the plants had become wild, blackened, and overgrown.

What are they called, he said. You have not told me.

Mendacium, she said as she opened the front door, for really he was making it too easy and it was thrilling to give him a clue.

The man at the hotel reception asked for her name. The name she gave was not her own.

21

ROSA IS RED, VIOLET IS BLUE

ALTHOUGH ROSA WAS thirty she still maintained many of the characteristics she had possessed as a child. She was red; she was a dragon, she was a tulip. This was the way she had been made. She was blood, she was fire. The men she took to her bed observed how, when she woke, her leg twitched and her skin itched; she was constantly restless. She spurned their advances for morning affections, instead pushing for the treadmill, the coffee, the shower—all the things that set her adrenaline pulsing, things she could control. She wanted everything NOW. She was a ball of rage. As a child, on a swing, her mother pushing her, and then as a teenager by herself, she had to go higher, HIGHer, HIGHER.

She had been rebellious at school. Her mother despaired of her and her father was forced to discipline her whenever he returned from work, handing out half-hearted punishments—stopping pocket money she didn't care about, or removing the plug from the tiny TV set she had in her bedroom, which blinked up and down and showed things through a fuzz of static snow. She learned graffiti from an early boyfriend and daubed the garden wall with obscenities, some of which her parents had never heard before and were horrified by when they looked them up online. She was expelled from a number of schools, regardless of the drop in general standards that went with each move, but she had a natural talent that rose above the need to revise and she dumbfounded many by gaining excellent results in her exams.

Violet, by contrast, approached thirty with many of her childhood characteristics, only with an added layer of nervousness and apprehension attached. She was blue; she was the ocean. She was a bluebell, she was a sapphire. This was the way she had been made. She was a crisp morning sky in January. She was fine by herself, preferring her own company and the lack of expectation that came with this solitude. She could amuse herself for hours with nothing more than pen and paper, or a book. When taken to a playground as a child she would try everything once, without emotion, giving as much time to the see-saw, which she loved, as to the roundabout, which she did not. She was then content to return home.

She was little trouble to her parents. When Violet woke early she would sit on her windowsill and watch the sun rise. She was happy for things to come later; she expected nothing. She sat up late with her parents in their beige and black armchairs that matched the curtains and furnishings in such a way that everything, when she squinted, swam together in the fading light before darkness truly fell. They played Scrabble, Trivial Pursuit, and an old, battered version of Operation with the heart missing, and she made them cups of weak tea, the same teabag dipped in each beige and black mug. She worked hard at school, studying at weekends, endlessly revising. It was a surprise to everyone when she failed her exams.

Rosa and Violet both arrived into adulthood with the same excitement and appetite for what was to come, though Violet's solitary youth had not prepared her for the trepidation she felt at being let loose in the world away from the comforts of her parents' home. Rosa simply forged ahead, going through men the way she went through packets of biscuits: with little thought for what she was doing, simply consuming what was put in front of her.

Violet went through packets of biscuits.

They both got good jobs, Violet overcoming the disappointment of her exam results with her pleasant demeanour, which held her in good stead in interview situations. They were always thinking, thinking; their minds whirring. Rosa's legs still jigged up and down, making everyone jittery at meetings she chaired. Violet began to feel that her inner thoughts had more control of her than she had over them and was often overcome, pulling the covers over her head as she slipped into bed in the early evening, an empty tub of Häagen-Dazs rolling across the floor.

They both, for a while, dated the same man. His name was Bellman, but Rosa called him Bellboy. This was meant as a term of derision, but he refused to take it as such. He could not make his choice, seeing qualities he liked in both women. He admired Rosa's ambition, her drive, her no-nonsense attitude, but equally adored Violet's humour, her stillness, the way she looked at the world. He alternated the days he met them, expecting to eventually favour one over the other, but he found at the end of each date with Rosa, he looked forward to the following day's meeting with Violet, and vice versa. When he did choose he settled on Rosa. When this didn't last (the decision to end the relationship obviously Rosa's) he wished he had chosen Violet. By then he had lost her number and, since they had always met on neutral ground and she, with a pathological fear of rapists and serial killers (not helped by the crime novels she read in rapid succession), had not told him where she lived or worked, he had no way of contacting her. He had seen Rosa's flat on the day they had met.

At various points in their lives Rosa and Violet met, in the loosest possible sense. They stood in line together at a super-

market checkout and Violet noticed the impatient way Rosa
tapped her fingers against the trolley. She also noticed the abun-
dance of wine bottles and ready meal lasagnes and cottage pies.
Two years later, Rosa saw Violet sitting on a park bench, a
Tupperware container in her lap containing the previous night's
leftovers (a mung bean and coconut curry), watching a squirrel
twirl the trunk of a tree, and for a moment envied her her calm,
her stillness. Twice they passed each other in the street and
looked directly into each other's eyes, but it was fleeting, as
these moments are, and barely registered with either of them.

Now, at opposite ends of this building, Rosa and Violet are
destined to meet properly for the first, and final time.

***

Rosa slams the Uber door. She has paid for this trip via her
smartphone and sees no reason to converse with the driver. She
says no goodbyes. The Uber driver, who has learned not to take
offence, watches Rosa stride toward the doors of the building,
her calves testifying to how often she wears heels of the height
she currently wears. She holds her bag in the way some women
do now, holding their arm out ahead of them, bent at the elbow,
as if they are marching against something, fists raised. The Uber
driver drives off, though he will later remember that he was here
at this building.

Violet is looking down from the optimistically named roof
garden. She works in this building and has come here simply to
look at the view. This is what she tells herself, but underneath
there is more and of course she is aware of it. It is true what
everyone says—people look like insects from up here, scurrying
around like trails of ants carrying colourful leaves. There is a
bucket of cigarette ends by her feet and it is nearly full. The
stench reaches her nostrils and she wonders how full the bucket
will need to be before someone takes the trouble to empty it. A

door slams below and the sound is louder than she expects it to be. She expected to be more removed from everyday life up here; she needed to feel more removed. The vertigo, also, is proving a challenge, with all of its sickening brain-swaying and none of its seductive call to submit. She has never liked heights; when she was a child she travelled with her parents to ruined castles and they climbed the turrets and towers, leaning over the feeblest of fences constructed in days when Health & Safety was not as strict as it is now. She rode the London Eye, but sat on the seat in the middle, and once the tops of nearby buildings were lost to view, she tried not to scream at her mother, who not only insisted on leaning on the glass to have her photo taken, but on leaning against the door to the capsule. Violet wished to be braver but her brain would not let her; she was powerless against biology. She lifts one of the cigarette butts from the bucket and presses it to her lips. She has never smoked and the smell that greets her does not make her want to start. She throws the butt over the edge of the building, because something must be sacrificed this way, and heads toward the thick fire exit door and the stairway back down.

The building is old and this stairway is purely functional, a featureless escape route on the side of the building with none of the carpeting and artwork that adorn the main central staircase. It has all the façade of a London hotel: visitors arrive in the plush reception area, climb the grand central stairs, and exit at various floors to each company's individual reception desk, to oak-lined meeting rooms and boardrooms. They do not pass through the doors that lead to the basic, open-plan areas where Violet works, and the grubby kitchenettes where she knocks elbows with colleagues simply by stirring her tea.

At first, Rosa and Violet pay each other little attention. They are passing on the stairwell just up from the first floor. Rosa has spent many minutes trying to explain to the vacuous receptionist that she would prefer a more discreet route than the central stairway as she is here to surprise her husband and does not wish to be seen on the way up by someone that may alert him of her arrival. The receptionist, whose name is Tiffani, has the receptionist's handbook seemingly etched onto her eyeballs and a gentle shaking of her head must surely signify the turning of virtual pages to find a suitable answer to Rosa's enquiry. The security of the building does not allow for surprises; does she have a name of a work colleague of her husband who could vouch for her and invite her up to the relevant floor? Then she can be allowed to proceed. Rosa, who has never entertained the idea of marriage, is at a loss so backs off, explaining that she will phone her husband and get him to come down if Tiffani is unable to help. Tiffani is not programmed to hear subtle snipes and simply nods and moves on to the next person in the queue. This man asks for something that requires Tiffani to turn her back momentarily. He nods Rosa in the direction of the door to the right of the gender-neutral bathrooms. She smiles gratefully and hurries over to the stairwell while Tiffani is otherwise engaged.

Violet has had time to descend twenty-three floors. She hears the low, clanking sound that is the start of what is to come, but pays it no mind. She has decided to return home and see how long it is before she is missed.

Rosa's mobile phone rings at this moment and, glancing at the screen to see who has rung, her mind clouds and she hears nothing, swiping the screen to ignore the call.

There is an ominous rumble that resonates through the walls. They both feel the stairway shudder beneath them. Violet notices Rosa's shoes. They are blood red with an impressive heel, the kind Violet would never wear. Still, she admires them greatly. As Rosa reaches out a hand to grab at the banister, the stairwell gives way beneath them and they plunge down with it. The noise around them intensifies.

When they are no longer falling, no longer being hit by debris, they lay still until the ringing in their ears lessens.

Am I dead? they think, and this is the first time they will think in rhythm like this. They are pressed together in a way that is intimate and that neither of them likes. A small amount of blood trickles down Rosa's forehead. Violet's face is pressed against Rosa's stomach; she can smell some kind of body wash or perfume. It is the sort that reeks out from make-up counters as she passes through department stores on the way to escalators that will take her to the café. They both try to move apart, but there is no room and they are stuck this way.

'Are you okay?' Rosa says. 'Can you move at all?' She says these things partly to herself, but it is hard to ignore the woman with her head pushed against her bladder.

Violet twists her neck to try to see Rosa's face, but everything is dark and there are still clouds of dust. They are two disembodied voices.

'I think I'm all right,' Violet says, 'but my leg is stuck.'

'Does it hurt?'

'It's just pressure. It's uncomfortable. What on earth happened?'

Rosa is not concerned about what has happened; she is only concerned about finding a way out of this situation. Mobile phones begin to ring around them. Violet tries to judge the distance of each ringtone from her ear. There are many to choose from, the usual sounds of ringing phones, but one is a child laughing and another a high-pitched voice saying 'Ex-squeeze me' over and again. It is an inappropriate sound for the occasion. Though Violet has worked in this building for some years, her phone does not ring. Rosa dropped her phone when she began to fall and if hers is one of those that rings she cannot see where it has gone. She is wedged in a gap and feels she is holding up the debris above her, a modern day Atlas, but reasons that this is unlikely to be possible.

There is a creak of metal and both women scream. Something rumbles and crashes. They can hear a man screaming in the distance in a pitch that is only subtly different from theirs. This screaming stops abruptly.

Rosa feels fear tighten its grip on her lungs. She has not been afraid of much in her life, but this may be beyond her. She resists the urge to fall apart.

'I'm Rosa,' she says, suddenly feeling the need to introduce herself.

Violet waits for a moment, then says, 'I'm Leah.' This feels like a moment when she should be someone different. Violet would not cope with this at all. Perhaps Leah will be able to find a way through. She feels a searing calm, which may be shock, but which she wishes to hold on to.

'Isn't this cosy,' Violet says, always one to mark an awkward encounter with an inane platitude.

'Isn't it just,' says Rosa, never one to make friends with women easily and unused to being in such intimate proximity with one. She is uncomfortable with where Violet's face is positioned and inches herself forward so that Violet is left with her face at Rosa's feet.

'What are you doing?' Violet says.

'I don't want your face there. It doesn't feel right,' Rosa says. 'Sorry. I have no idea. I just feel I should be doing something.'

'Shouldn't we keep still?' Violet is imagining all sorts of scenarios; she finds now that she has no wish for her life to be extinguished. 'I expect we should. Keep still, that is. Yes.'

Violet tries to follow her own advice, though she is bruised all over and her head throbs. She feels she should make some effort to free her leg, but doesn't wish to dislodge anything that may come crashing down on them. Her mind, which is thinking only of practicalities at this point, presents the image of a nice cup of tea.

'Typical,' she says.

'I fail to see what part of any of this is typical,' says Rosa, already impatient to be stuck in this way with such a buffoon.

'It's just that... well... even stuck in this disaster movie I'm still craving a nice cup of tea. I really am that dull.'

She knows instinctively what her role will be in this movie. She will be the weak and feeble one holding the others back, dithering and whining, until she refuses to squeeze through a tight space and is left behind.

Rosa is quiet for a moment. Violet mentally twiddles her thumbs.

'I rather think this calls for a coffee,' says Rosa.

'I've thought for some time I needed to slow down,' Rosa says, breaking a momentary silence. 'I didn't think this would be the way.'

Violet titters in the way she does when people talk to her and she doesn't know what to say in response.

'I've just turned thirty,' Rosa says. 'No big deal, of course, but the passing of a decade makes one think. I need to be calmer—I'm so damn het up all the time. It can't be good for me. Medically. I signed for meditation classes, such a cliché. Wishy-washy nonsense, of course.' She had been able to see the cathedral clock through the window and had kept looking up at it, ever more frequently, until she thought she had meditated time into stopping. 'I did five weeks, which for me is really sticking at something.' Five weeks, until the compulsion to scream with frustration mid-session overwhelmed her and she had felt it best to leave before she acted on it. 'Colossal waste of money, of course. No refunds. Just like a gym. A mind gym.'

She smiles at her own joke.

'I'm twenty-nine,' Violet says. 'Clinging on to it, barely. It's my birthday next month. I never used to mind being on my own'. As a child, as a teenager, she had only had to get up, go to school, and come home again. Nothing else required. Now everything needed some kind of social interaction. 'I'm just so bloody mousy. I just want a pinch of self-confidence. I drove to a pub, miles away, of course, where nobody could possibly know me... not that anyone knows me. I signed up for karaoke. Is that a cliché as well? I don't know. I sang "All By Myself".' Because although she is trying to better herself, she still knows who she is and is unafraid of the irony.

Rosa laughed. 'And how did it go?'

'There was polite applause, but nothing compared to the rowdy cheers that greeted the next singer, who was barely in tune but wore next to nothing.' Violet had gone to Debenhams the next day, edged her way through the lingerie section, as always—nearest the door—to the nightlife section, which, it had to be said, had an awful lot in common with the lingerie section. She had decided it was all a step too far.

'Do you work here?' Rosa says. 'I was on my way up to see my lover's wife.' Calling him her lover makes it seem seductive and amorous, but it isn't. 'He's just a man I've been sleeping with for too long. I'm not even that into him.' She isn't sure she had realised this until she said it out loud to someone else. 'I know his wife—he's made sure I do. He invites me to functions they are both attending, so that he can steal a hand inside my skirt in a stationery cupboard or in the lift, then introduces me to her knowing that he is fucking both of us.' In her basest moments it is titillating, but mostly, at functions he takes her to, she spends most of the time drinking wine in a corner, talking to some sad loser who is trying to hit on her, while over his shoulder she can see her *lover* fondling his wife.

Violet can see that Rosa's life is infinitely more exciting than hers, but equally this is not the type of person she is aspiring to be.

'I despise myself more often than not,' Rosa is saying, 'when I think of him. So, I figured I would tell his sanctimonious wife, who, of course, has done nothing wrong other than marry him, but why should I let that stop me? He will be angry, of course, and will have nothing to do with me again, wanting, as he quite rightly should, to save his pathetic sham of a marriage.' He has freckles around his neckline and across his shoulders and Rosa tries not to look at them when he fucks her because that is something real, something unseen across a Skype call, not hinted at in a filthy text. 'God, I'm so weak, so shallow. Of course, it will solve nothing, there'll always be another man and I *do not* attract the right men, and the confrontation will likely destroy my career.' But she has examined her cards and decided to play them, though there is no doubt she does not hold a winning hand. 'I knew something would stop me, though, I felt it in my water, as my mother used to say. I wasn't quite expecting something as extreme as this.'

Violet is nudging with her nose at the tip of Rosa's stiletto, trying to dislodge the shoe in the hope of retrieving it in the madness that will surely accompany any rescue attempt.

'Are you even listening to me?' Rosa says. She feels the shoe fall, and even in this situation feels a little of the relief that normally comes at the end of the day when she removes them.

'I was going to jump,' Violet says, tucking the shoe into her armpit. 'Except, of course, I wasn't. But I went up there, and the thought was there, in the back of my mind. And, of course, I felt ridiculous when I was up there. I don't want the last thing I properly look at to be a bucket of cigarette butts. I just feel so *fucking* insignificant.'

Violet uses the f-word because Rosa used it, not because it is something she does, but because the thing she does is to force herself to be someone that she thinks another person wants her to be: on the rare occasions she dates, when she meets people like Rosa, when she goes home to see her parents. But her perceptions are off every time, because men don't date her for long, people like Rosa don't want to be her friend, and her parents don't really invite her—she just shows up.

'We could look back on this moment with fondness,' Rosa says. 'When we are forty. Who knows what the next decade will bring. Perhaps this is the time of our lives.'

'Fuck,' Violet says.

'Quite,' Rosa says. 'I raise a metaphorical glass to another decade. Here's to the future.'

Violet raises both hands in something approximating a toast. When she puts them down again she knocks against something.

'I've found your phone,' she says. They hear scrabbling sounds and voices calling, are assured that help is on its way. Violet pushes the phone into Rosa's pocket. They lay quietly together, waiting. But the rescuers disturb something. There are panicked shouts, and the building shudders around them. Violet grabs on to Rosa's leg, and Rosa is, for once, grateful for the contact.

'Well, it was nice to meet you,' Violet says.

'Likewise,' says Rosa, and is surprised to mean it.

The weight of the building shifts; the stairwell descends further and crushes down on them. Rosa is Violet. Violet is Rosa. This new woman is the best of them both. When she is pulled from the wreckage she cannot think of a name to give and so she doesn't give one. Then when asked again she calls herself Leah. It is not hard to fake being disorientated, groggy. The central staircase has collapsed; a few internal walls have fallen. Casualties are limited. Violet's work colleagues have gathered in a group, and the wife of the man Rosa has been sleeping with is also there. Leah, who is both Rosa and Violet (and is, of course, wearing Rosa's shoes), scans their faces. There is a moment's glimmer of recognition from each of them but not enough to make them stop and call out to her. This new woman is not Rosa, and is not Violet.

Leah senses she cannot go back to the lives she had before. She walks away from the devastation, fumbling in her pocket for her phone, scrolling down until she finds the name 'Bellboy', hovering over his number. She thinks it would be worth her time making this call.

As Leah Bellman approaches forty she has many of the characteristics that dominated her early life. She is fire, she is water. She is blood, she is the ocean. She has a rage inside her, but is able to calm herself down. When she takes her child (Rosa Violet Bellman, to the consternation of her father who was overruled when objecting to his daughter bearing the names of two former girlfriends) to the playground and pushes her on the swing, her daughter must go higher, HIGHer, HIGHER. But when she is told it is time to leave, she accepts this calmly. She does not make a fuss.

22

SEMI-DETACHED

WE ARE the spirits who muffle the cries of those who are semi-detached.

We do our best to preserve your dignity. We live inside your walls, in spaces long forgotten.

A running tap will not drown out your angry words; the raised volume on the TV will not fool anyone. They cannot mask the crockery smash, the skin slap, the glass shatter.

We seek out the places where neighbours hold glasses to walls. We cluster there to scupper those spies. But they should not despise us, for we do the same for them.

We gather together so your screams don't penetrate through wallpaper, plasterboard, bricks and mortar. We extinguish those expletives, the ones you so rarely dare to use. We are the insulation against your private moments reaching the ears of your neighbours. And yes, we are there for *those* private moments too. We stifle those cries the most; your neighbours have no wish to hear them.

At night, when you sleep, we come out from the walls and gather at your fevered brow. We gently vibrate against your skin, soothing, calming, pushing the bad thoughts away.

Oh, you think you are alone in your sorrows, but we have seen them all before. You are no different to us from the man, the woman, the boy, the girl who lived here years ago. If we are honest, we have a hard time recognising the change from generation to generation.

We have seen their joys too, as we see yours. Do not forget when things go wrong that there are also moments of joy. These we do not cover, these we let run free. We are only there to hide your misery, to quash the bitter words you say in the heat of an affray.

We want no thanks for it; it is just what we do.

We are the spirits who muffle the cries of those who are semi-detached.

23

SMOKE SIGNALS

THEY ARE ON THE HILLSIDE. Clouds gather in vicious shapes in the distance, but this is not something that will stop them in what they are doing. Yuta stands and shuffles his feet in the dirt, thrusting them forward and back, making the footprints he will leave when he is older. He watches, with longing, two boys his own age kicking a ball between them in the valley below. The distance makes them seem like something apart from him, something he could never reach. His great-grandfather is building a tower of twigs and bracken. It is a beautiful thing, each twig carefully placed to take the weight of those that will follow.

'You must listen to your great-grandfather,' his mother has said. 'He has lived many years. He has much he can tell you.'

But Yuta has little patience and much energy. Poppa Lukka moves so slowly. Yuta's legs burn with the desire to run.

'We must light this small fire first,' Lukka is saying. 'It shows that I am teaching you, that my signals are to be ignored.'

Lukka knows that Yuta's mind is elsewhere, but this is the way his people signal to each other, how it has always been done. It is a dying art, and one he wishes to preserve.

Things are changing, the pace of it unstoppable. Aeroplanes

come and drop plastic bags of clothes that people in other countries no longer want and the children in the village run around in brightly coloured T-shirts bearing writing they cannot understand. Yuta wears one of these T-shirts now. Red, with a picture of a skull that appears to be yawning. Lukka's eyesight is failing. He believes this to be a gift from the gods, because there is much he no longer wishes to see. Yuta is his youngest great-grandchild, his last chance to teach some of what he has learned.

Lukka grabs Yuta by the shoulder and spins him to face him. The boy is startled and loses his balance momentarily so that Lukka has to hold him up.

'I know you wish to run down this hill, Yuta,' he says. 'You *should* run. You should run fast until you trip and fall and roll the rest of the way because you are young and can do these things and the fall will not hurt you. But when you need to warn someone, this is quicker than even you can run. I cannot run with you, Yuta. How I wish I could. But I can give you this, I can teach you this.'

Yuta looks into his eyes and Lukka sees something soften there.

'Of course, Poppa,' Yuta says. 'I'm sorry.' This man has always been in his life. He does not wish to offend him.

Lukka shows how the positioning of the twigs affects the direction the plumes of smoke will take. He shows him techniques to break the trails of smoke so individual shapes are created. Yuta follows him obediently up and down the hill as he shows him the different positions fires can be lit and what these positions signify.

Despite himself, Yuta finds his interest growing. He tries hard to remember the signals for individual letters of the alphabet, though some of the differences are so subtle he is sure any messages he were to try to send would be impossible to understand. He senses a desperation in Poppa Lukka to pass these things on and resolves to try hard to take these things in. His great-grandfather has always been kind to him; there will be time enough to kick a ball.

'Would they not hear us if we shout?' Yuta asks, looking across at the nearest hillside and the dwellings dotted upon it.

'We are a tribe who give thanks to our gods in songs and chanting. The voice is to be prized. It is not to be wasted hollering from one hilltop to another.'

Yuta smiles at this. He has trouble himself catching Poppa Lukka's frail voice and cannot believe his great-grandfather could ever holler.

'What can we do if it rains and we need to send a signal?' Yuta asks then.

Lukka frowns at his great-grandson. He despairs at the loss of the old ways. What is this boy being taught? But he is keen; he asks questions and seems to have forgotten his desire to kick a ball about.

'When it rains there is no danger,' Lukka says. 'It does not rain often, and when it does it is a gift from the gods. Everything stops and we give thanks. We dance. We celebrate.'

Yuta loves these rain dances. The whole tribe gathers and dances the way he does: free, uninhibited, with no discernible rhythm.

'Have you ever used the warning signals, Poppa?' Yuta asks, his face serious.

'I have,' Lukka says. 'When your grandfather was only a few years older than you are now.'

There is a tradition of stories in his village, but Yuta sometimes thinks the best stories are denied him, nods across tables between the elders of the family when certain subjects are raised. Yuta has heard little about his grandfather Echo.

Lukka is staring into the middle distance. Yuta does not know whether to press further.

'Was there much danger, Poppa?'

Lukka remembers lighting those fires all too well. The world had started to speed up around them, their way of life left far behind. Others came to steal their crops, then their land and, sometimes, their women. They weren't from any one place, but the tribes called them Rivals. They wore trousers and shirts, and boots on their feet. They carried weapons.

At the height of it all, Lukka had seen the danger sign on the nearest hillside, the plumes of smoke rising behind showing that the village also burned. Lighting the fires on his hill to warn those to the north, he had run down this very incline that Yuta longed to run down. On and on, his blood pounding until he tasted it in his throat. Rivals rampaged through the village, leering grins on their faces, swinging their weapons. He had seen a young man in trousers and shirt dragging a screaming girl from her hut, pulling her by her hair. Rushing to her rescue, Lukka had clenched his fist ready to strike the man and then the man had turned his head and struck Lukka without lifting a finger. It was Echo.

'There has been much danger,' Lukka says. 'It has passed now.'

Now they are revered. Men come with cameras to film their way of life. These men are still Rivals of sorts, encroaching on the everyday way of things, but the battles are behind them.

It was all a long time ago. He must learn to forgive. Echo was young, impressionable, easily influenced by others. The children Echo fathered are fine men and women, and they in turn have fathered children such as Yuta, who have delighted him in his old age.

'So many questions,' Lukka says, smiling. 'We still have much to do.'

———

It has been a long day. Yuta and Lukka return to Lukka's hut. They give thanks to their gods and go to sleep. Yuta sleeps well and does not stir until the dawn sun appears. Lukka does not respond when Yuta calls to him. His skin is cold.

Yuta sits for a while with the body of his great-grandfather, then goes out onto the hillside. He gathers twigs and bracken. He lights a fire at the point on the hill that signifies a death. Then, at the highest point of the hill he sends five plumes of smoke into the sky and disrupts the smoke of each so they spell out 'Lukka'. The smoke blurs his vision and at first he thinks this is what causes the tears to fall, but he is crying for his Poppa Lukka, who he loves and will never see again.

The villagers start to come from the valley below. The women go into Lukka's hut to prepare his body. Yuta hears them begin to sing the songs that will see his great-grandfather into the next life. The men of the village come to Yuta to express their sorrow. The oldest of them, who still knows how to send signals by smoke, offers to take over, but Yuta refuses.

'Poppa Lukka taught me,' he says through his tears. 'I will do it.'

Soon he can see in the distance a trail of people from outlying villages, come to pay their respects. The elders tell him there is no longer any need to signal. He sees fires lit on surrounding hill-sides, his great-grandfather's name sent into the sky.

He snuffs his fires out as Lukka has taught him, so the smoke is extinguished. He goes to the hut. Inside, his great-grandfather is still being attended to; the songs the women sing are sweet and sorrowful. Yuta places his hands on the outside of the hut.

'Come run with me, Poppa,' he says. His great-grandfather's spirit will be guided on its way later, when the sun starts to set, but for now Yuta has need of it.

He turns and runs down the hill to the valley below. He runs fast, so fast he feels he might trip and fall and roll the rest of the way. But he is young and can do these things. The fall will not hurt him.

24

———————

WHITE NOISE

HE WAS A TREE: sturdy, unmoving. But trees had the luxury of moving their branches; this he was denied.

His family were birds alighting, daily visits, much flapping of wings. His mother filled him in on family and friends—every little detail. His father gave him football scores, weather reports. His brother talked of television, parties, girls.

Do not tell me these things, he thought. These people are lost to me.

Is there nothing they can give me, he thought, to make this stop?

And always his family's endless chatter. He knew they meant nothing by it, but it hurt him to hear of things he could no longer take part in. He wished to tune their voices out.

I am not who I was, he thought. Why must *they* stay the same?

He learned instead to focus on the noises they made. His mother rubbed her hands gently back and forth across his sheet (perhaps his arm), this, the sound of the sea. His brother's leg urgently jiggled in that impatient way he had. His father, who weighed too much post-retirement, took laboured breaths. He built this orchestra up, working with what he had, pulling it together and creating a symphony.

He had no choice but to compose his own pieces, no run of sounds he heard would ever suggest a tune he knew. His attention moved from one noise to another, then pulled back and listened to them all as a whole.

The pieces were often harried, insistent. His brother's leg moved fast. The wind caused the blinds to knock, knock, knock. There was a background of sirens. They were like the discordant jazz pieces his father would play to him and his brother when they were young.

Close your eyes and listen, he would say, and the three of them would sit back in their chairs, eyes closed. He remembered the static noise the needle made on the vinyl. This was the sound he looked for.

So he became adept at tuning his family's voices out, and if his own voice in his head berated him for doing this, then he tuned that out too.

They will understand, he argued with himself. If I am ever able to tell them, they will understand. They will see. Like this they are a comfort to me.

And his eyes would fill with tears, only they did not.

He listened to the pieces he composed and believed himself to be content.

There were words that got through. It was hard to ignore an 'I love you, son' whispered hard and fast in his ear.

At night, the knock, knock of the blinds and the clack, clack of trains carried across the night-time distance, and the muted whispers of the nurses at their station like the static sound of a needle on vinyl.

25

IT WAS SOMETHING HER GRANDMOTHER SAID

KHLOE IS SLUGGISH, tired. The dregs of the previous night rest in her intestines; her head semi-swims. Half-closing sleep-crusted eyes, she piles high a teaspoon with coffee and tips it in an 'I love the 80s' mug (ironic this—she is a 90's child and has a disdain of the decade that preceded her birth).

Mildew stains seep down walls creating accidental artwork; with their own graceful curves they reach to the floor.

Khloe loads another teaspoon with sugar. Lack of sleep and surfeit of alcohol provide the necessary brain instructions to move wrist from right to left. She continues this mockery show until only a few sugar specks remain. *Might as well. Hardly worth putting it back in the bag.* She tips them in.

Khloe makes for the lounge. The carpet has a damp dog smell when she dips her nose to it. The sofa sinks below what is comfortable when she plonks her arse down. She holds the coffee mug with both hands, warming her skin.

Through the window the world walks by. Her mould-strewn net curtains are crumpled and shoved in the mahogany unit under the TV. She resented their cloying constraints as she struggled to squint through them, and tore them down the day she moved in. Now she has free TV-screen access to real life, her own reality show; though she is brought up short by a look to camera, the intrusive glance from the occasional passer-by.

The girl upstairs plays an album Khloe possesses and she puts it on, trying to match up the tracks. This girl appears to be in a lesbian relationship, considering the alternating sounds of love-making and argument that seep through the ceiling tiles. Khloe has pondered this option (with considerable naïvety, weighing it up like she might a change of hairstyle), but reasons that women are bitches and men easier to control; using herself and her own experiences as a reference point has clouded her judgement somewhat.

The abrasive sneer of the door buzzer sounds. Khloe spills splashes of coffee on already stained sweatpants. She stops the CD playing and the song continues on upstairs, muffled and distant.

In the front-door spyhole, Meena leers, a lone nasal moun-tain. Khloe has half a mind not to let her in. When they were kids, too young to be left, their mothers would leave them alone in the house and tell them to drop to their knees and crouch behind sofas and doorways if anyone came knocking. *Ignore 'em when they call through the letterbox; they're just trying to scare you. They can't get in.* Khloe unconsciously starts to bend her knees now, wishing to hide. Left alone she will swipe through the contacts list on her phone, wondering who she can call. She makes half-hearted arrangements, meets up ten or fifteen minutes late, then is surly and uncommunicative, wishing to be by herself.

As kids, Khloe and Meena did it all: ran riot, laughed and cried, flashed their private parts at each other to check they weren't deformed in some way. They racked up huge phone bills for their fathers as they shed tears, whispered sordid secrets about boyfriends. They vowed to be friends forever. Meena wanted to slice their fingers and mingle their blood; they had used table knives that weren't sharp enough, still screaming at the touch of steel on skin. In the end they rubbed squirted blobs of tomato ketchup into their fingers.

You two can talk the torso from a donkey, never mind its hind legs, her mother used to say. All those wasted vowels and consonants, compacted together into inanity: Big Brother, X Factor, soaps and celebrity gossip, all the things they wanted from life. Getting together now they are a pair of broken records, discussing the same old shit. Khloe couldn't give a rat's arse about any of it.

Meena has dropped by on her way back from the shops. 'Can I use your loo?' she says when Khloe opens the door, brushing past her, planting a fake kiss against Khloe's ear as she goes. The sound nearly deafens her.

Khloe sits on her bed and listens to the piss-cascade splashing into the bowl. In the bedroom the furniture is mismatched, wooden and faded. The wardrobe door does not shut properly. In the chest of drawers: a T-shirt and a pale blue pair of knickers from the previous tenant. She has often pondered what is significant about these garments, why these alone should be left. She doesn't use the drawer, and the things are still in there. She has a table outside the toilet: on it a bottle of vodka and an egg cup. She fills the egg cup each morning and downs the vodka before she cleans her teeth. This is how Khloe starts her day.

She wonders if Meena needed the toilet so desperately she had no choice but to drop by; imagines her cross-legged in frustration and thinking of Khloe as her last resort; pictures her calculating how long she needs to stay to seem polite.

Meena comes out without washing her hands and plops herself on the chair opposite the bed. She wears her hair pulled back tight from her face and casually swept up because this is how the singer Adele wears it. But Adele styles her hair like this when she is out for a stroll, popping out for some milk. Meena wears her hair like this all the time.

'I'll get you a tea,' Khloe says.

'Thanks.'

'Window shopping, was it?' Khloe says, because Meena has no bags.

'Yeah, then I remembered I got windows, so I thought I'd come see you.'

An old joke, often repeated.

'Ba boom,' Khloe says, rapping her knuckles on the draining board.

Meena talks about shops she's been to, people she's seen who Khloe might know. Khloe nods and tunes her out, dips a teabag in a chipped mug that says 'Happy Easter'.

Conversation stalls. Khloe arches her back and her bones crack. Meena makes a dry, clicking sound with her tongue that grates on Khloe's nerves. Her life feels as if she is permanently in a queue on the phone, with no idea of how long that queue is, waiting for something to happen, not sure when it will start, everything she has ready to say fading away from her as she waits, and a voice saying '*You are in a queue, please continue to hold*' at thirty second intervals, making her blood pressure rise.

'Where's the cat?' Meena asks, barely twisting her head around, not really interested.

'I let him out now,' Khloe says.

She had come back from the RSPCA Animal Rescue Centre with a cat, jet black and jumpy. Released from its box it scurried under the slim space under the wardrobe and refused to come out. It stayed there for days. Nervous and flighty, staring back at her with wide eyes.

Khloe named him Tipsy ('*Not very masculine*'—this from her mum); the mixture of nervousness and vulnerability seemed to suggest the name. She was wary of opening doors to let him out so kept him indoors for weeks, using the grimy tray of the shower cubicle as a litter tray. Khloe preferred baths anyway, though now she had to turn and have her head at the tap end to avoid the unpleasant smell. Tipsy warmed to her eventually and now walked tall, as if he had crept out at night to attend AA meetings and was now fully reformed. He sidled around her legs, moulting hair against her trousers, and scratched at the door to be let out. Khloe had panicked the first time he leaped the wall of her small concrete yard (weeds the only greenery), but he came back at night and when he wished to be fed. She had known men who behaved the same.

Meena pulls at a piece of fabric coming loose from the chair; though it is threadbare and stained Khloe resents this disregard for her stuff. She can feel the strain of trying to recapture their teenage exuberance, of trying to patch up the fraying connections that linger between them. She harbours a wish that Meena will move away so the severing will be complete and no one will be to blame. When Meena tired of Khloe as a teenager she switched chairs in class. Khloe thinks of this suddenly. Walking into Chemistry one day, sticker-crossed satchel swinging, and Meena sat at one of the long benches in the middle of the classroom, between two other girls she was friendly with. Khloe stopped in the middle of the gangway; the girl behind walked into her. Meena and her two friends laughing, whispering theatrically to each other behind cupped hands. Khloe sat at the desk she usually shared with Meena, their initials scraped into the wood with metal compasses. Sat there alone and for the rest of the year, gouging away at the M, finding it hard to concentrate on anything the teacher said. Meena angled only slightly back from her, so that if Khloe turned to look at the board she could see her at the edge of her eye, a cloud in the corner, a bloodshot pupil. In other lessons, without the two girls, Meena stayed put beside her. They carried on as before and never mentioned it. Khloe has not forgotten it.

Now Meena has Paul, and this has affected them again. Khloe sees how Meena is different with men, creates a persona for them. Khloe carries on regardless, making no concessions, hoping they'll take her as she is. They do for a bit, but it grates after a while and by then Khloe has usually lost interest.

Khloe is bored of looking at this reflection of her teenage self. She wishes, too, for something to happen. She has always been someone who does things for a reaction: talking loudly on a crowded train; opening her window on a still, sunny day when she has music blaring; saying *what the fuck are you looking at?* to random people in the street who are not looking at anything.

Khloe is a person who says things like this: 'Look, Meena, I've got something to tell you.' She leans forward and puts her hands together. 'I'll just say it. I slept with Paul. Just once, not that that helps. And it meant something, yeah, because it's crap to say it didn't. But it only meant what it was. A one-time thing. That's all. It was ages ago. I should have said at the time, but...'

Khloe says these things because the day has become dull. When she checks Meena's face for a reaction, there is nothing there to read.

'It's fine.' Meena's lips tighten. 'I know all about it. He told me.'

'I didn't...' Khloe falters; she has never slept with Paul, has never wanted to. 'I didn't know he'd said anything. I can't think why he would.'

'No, I don't suppose you can.'

Meena leaves the sentence hanging.

'I...' Khloe feels the coffee slosh in her stomach. 'What did he tell you?'

'Everything,' Meena says. 'So there's nothing you can add.' There is a narrowing of the eyes from both, battle lines drawn.

'I can't believe he told you,' Khloe says. 'We agreed not to.'

'Can we not talk about it?' Meena says. 'I suppose I should be grateful you've told me at last, but please don't expect me to act like you've done me a favour.'

'It's best to know what he's really like.'

'Then why leave it so long to tell me?'

'I don't know.' Khloe chews at a flake of skin coming away from her lip. 'Shouldn't you be yelling at me, tearing at my hair?'

'Oh, what does it matter? It's only sex.' Meena thuds her coffee cup down on the floor. 'It's not like you ever put any emotion into your encounters with men. Shall we have another coffee?'

'I'm not sure how to take that.'

'Milk and sugar, like always?'

Khloe smiles thinly.

'If it was a stranger,' Meena says, 'you wouldn't be talking as if it meant anything, as if you were in love. Would you?'

Khloe had only ever loved one man really, and he had gone home to someone else at the end of every day.

'No. Of course not. Look, I don't really like him that much.'

'Well, what does it matter then?'

She had never believed this man when he said there'd be a right time to leave the girl he went home to. Khloe has, at least, never been gullible. She never spared this girl a thought, other than to think she should have had a tighter grip on her man. She would fantasise about her finding out, coming at her all guns blazing. She had almost looked forward to it.

'Did I tell you about Aunt Rhona?' Meena is saying. 'She's booked a three-month cruise. I can't even remember where she's going. I was too jealous to listen.'

'You do get jealous then?' Khloe says.

'When people have things that I don't, yes.'

Khloe is suddenly weary, swamped by the feeling that perhaps she and Meena never really liked each other. They just sat next to each other in primary school and started talking, fated by nothing more than seating plans to be joined at the hip.

'Why do you always get to be the one that keeps conversations going?' Meena says.

'I just think we should talk about it.' The dregs of Khloe's coffee are starting to skin over. She swishes them about. 'I would want to know what went on.'

'You would,' Meena says. 'But I don't need to know. It's not important. Flailing about in bed isn't what makes a life.'

'You never were any good at Biology.'

'Yes, well,' Meena says, getting to her feet. 'Thank goodness it didn't come to that.'

She goes into the kitchen and rinses her cup in the sink.

'He doesn't even like you, you know,' she says, her back to Khloe.

'Imagine how he is with the ones he does like,' Khloe says.

Meena's arms pause. Khloe knows she has her then. Meena drops the mug in the sink, hard enough to break it. No more Happy Easter.

'We should have pierced the skin, that time,' Meena says. 'Mixed our blood.'

Left alone, Khloe practises the breathing she has been taught— deep breaths in and out, concentrating on the feel of her feet on the floor. She listens to the noises in the room: the thrum of the traffic passing by, the electric fizz and hum of the 21st century, the CD playing on upstairs—still her skin crawls.

She stares at the pattern in the carpet until her eyes cross. She picks up the phone.

A few doors down a woman stands on the doorstep smoking, a tattered dressing gown pulled around her, and with the kind of weather-beaten face that suggests a couple of decades extra to what she has probably experienced. This is Neighbourhood Watch: a beady eye in everyone's business. Khloe doesn't meet her eye, doesn't nod a greeting. This community has no hub.

It has rained, briefly. The pavement is wet, littered with

skinny pink worms as if some half-arsed Medusa was shedding her hair. Khloe makes no allowances for these creatures, letting her boots fall where they fall.

They meet in a hotel lobby. It fits in with the fabricated story they have independently concocted, a story Khloe is starting to believe. She has been here once before, conducting some vox pop interviews at a bank's Annual General Meeting, wasting time on some job centre-suggested government initiative. Before Paul arrives, Khloe enquires about room availability and prices, though Paul will have to pay if it comes to that. The woman behind the reception desk looks at her like she is making assumptions about Khloe that are wrong, but along the right lines. Khloe goes over to sit in the leather sofas opposite the reception desk and defiantly meets her gaze. She picks at her fingernails, slicing off crescent clippings and dropping them on the shiny floor tiles, leaving traces of her DNA around.

Paul grins when he sees Khloe. 'Well,' he says, throwing himself into the sofa opposite. 'Here's a thing. Two lies entwined.'

Khloe has never liked him, he is not attractive to her, but as he says the word *entwined* she feels the pull of the hotel rooms above. He looks like a hundred other guys: short cropped hair and a pub-ready grin. He walks with his hands tucked into the waistband of his underwear in the way young men do, as if they have a rash they must surreptitiously scratch.

'What made you say it?' he says.

Khloe shrugs. 'What about you?' she says. 'What did you tell her?'

Paul pushes his arse forward and slouches down in his seat. He is constantly looking about, catching everyone's eye.

'I said you threw yourself at me. Came to the house when you knew she was out. Stripped off in front of me. Said you were pretty desperate.'

'You told her we fucked in her house?'

'She didn't ask anything. She didn't seem all that surprised,' he says. 'You screwed her men before?'

'No.' Khloe fights the urge to spit in his face. He smiles at a girl tottering by on impractical heels, face trowelled with make-up. The girl feigns shyness and smiles in a way she must practise in the mirror.

'It'll eat away at her,' Khloe says. 'It'll come back to bite you in the end.'

Paul shrugs. 'Totally worth the risk. I didn't know if it was a long-term thing then.'

'You were living in her house.'

'Yeah, still am. And paying rent. It's no biggie to move.' Khloe sees now that he has chosen this hotel so she would feel out of place. He puts his feet up on the lip of the magazine-strewn coffee table between them. He stares right at her, grin spreading like sewage. She looks down at his feet. There is a hole starting to form on the sole of his left shoe, and he has trod in something: gum or dog shit, and a streak of it smears his sock, visible through the hole.

'God, it was just something to say,' he says, 'to shift you from her life. She deserves better than you. Plus, it made the day interesting.'

Khloe winces to hear him voice what she has thought. God's cruel trick on her then—or no, the Devil's. *'The Devil's touché'* was something her grandmother said. *Don't mess with the Devil, he always has a comeback.* Her grandmother said many things, pointless sayings nobody else had ever heard, but they cut into Khloe, saw right into her.

Khloe gets to her feet. She thinks about going. Then she walks over to Paul and sits beside him. He seems amused. She can smell his aftershave.

'Well,' she says, 'Meena already thinks we've been together. She didn't seem that bothered.'

She touches the lapels of his jacket, brushes her fingers

against his chin. Though he has recently shaved she can feel the scrape of the bristles he's missed. 'She's almost giving us permission.'

He laughs then, unable to keep it in. 'You can't help yourself, can you? You make it so easy. Meena gets you, you know, what you're like. She says she knew you when you spelled your name right.'

Khloe is sensitive to the insult. The 'C' changed to a 'K', quite the done thing at the time. She has known men called Kallum, Khris. She changed the name properly, on credit cards, benefit claims, everything—it was all official. She finds she misses the uncluttered curve of the 'C'.

Paul stands and looks her up and down. He shakes his head. 'You'd be pretty prick-defeating, babes.'

Khloe watches him leave. Meena is standing in the doorway and Khloe knows she has seen everything. Meena gives Paul a smile as he approaches; she lightly touches the lapel of his shirt, a mirror of Khloe's clumsy attempt at seduction. She does naturally what Khloe needs to force. Meena doesn't even need to look at Khloe—she has made her point. She links arms with Paul and they leave. He cannot resist a twist of the neck, a condescending wink.

Khloe looks across the hotel lobby and catches her reflection in the glass behind the reception desk. Nervous and flighty, staring back at her with wide eyes.

SPREADING THE CHAOS

HE IS TAKING groceries into the house, an obedient little puppy; his wife directing him as if this is something that needs supervision.

Out the window she yells, 'Oi, shit brains. I've had the abortion, so screw you, have it all your way.'

He looks on with a bemused expression, a lost little boy, unsure which way to turn. His wife punches him on the shoulder; still he holds her gaze.

She winds the window up, gives a mock salute, and drives away.

She has never seen this man before. This is just something she does. Spreading the chaos.

A MAN, OUT WALKING

HE WALKS AT SPEED, this man, heading toward the cliff tops. Perhaps he feels vulnerable alone and the velocity makes him seem immune to whatever danger he perceives. He is not dressed in a runner's apparel; he does not have a dog or a walking companion. Maybe he does not make friends easily, or perhaps he had many friends and has now lost them all.

At the end of his town is a steep slope up to the tops of the cliffs and the hills beyond. This slope is a barometer of his fitness. When he first climbed it he felt breathless, needed to pause halfway up with his hands on his hips, fighting the urge to bend double to catch his breath. Now he walks here regularly he does not slow, strides up in easy steps, feeling the pull in his leg muscles.

At the top of this slope the town is spread out before him in its entirety. Maybe if he once had a wife, a daughter, he would sense their absence from the homes he sees spread before him. Maybe he turns quickly away from the view because of this.

He veers left, following the cliff path. There is a dip and a playing field below. This has been used as a location in a big Hollywood movie, but was laden with so many special effects he struggled to recognise it when he saw the film. He can see a woman walking a dog ahead of him on his path, and on another a solitary jogger. Sometimes he does not see a soul and this makes him feel lonely, but he prefers this feeling to the one he gets when he sees too many people heading toward him.

There is a bench on which he sits for a moment, because he has always done so. He reads the inscription on it, though he knows it by heart. Maybe he used to walk up here with his wife. Maybe they sat here together.

He stares out at the horizon as he often does, trying to discern shapes and colours that could be another land mass. He doesn't know if he should be able to see one from here, but there is always a darker shade of grey dotted along the horizon as if it could be the outline of hills. Perhaps it is just the sun reflecting back an image of the hills he sits on and a tiny dot of it is a reflection of him, sitting there with his arm outstretched and his hand shading his eyes.

He gets up again. The woman with the dog he saw earlier is now nearly level with him. He knows this woman. She nods to him and greets him by name without breaking her stride. She stopped once when her dog jumped up at him and he fell backward into brambles. The name the woman greets him with is not his own. She calls him Bill when his name is Ben and he does not know if this is done with intention, as a joke, or is the simple confusion of two names so often paired together. Because he doesn't know, he doesn't correct her. Perhaps this does not concern him; perhaps he would like to be someone else.

He smells the scents of flowers as he passes them. He knows them only by colour and shape. He thinks of his grandfather, who knew the names of every plant, flower, and tree; who had enrolled him as a member of a horticultural society, for which he received a burgundy enamel badge, and bought him books about plants. But he showed interest only in the badge, and his membership was not renewed. Maybe he would have liked a young daughter who nagged at him until he cleared a patch of the garden just for her. Maybe it would have saddened him the way the garden was abandoned and overgrown with weeds as she got older, because even when he tried to clear it for her she would say, 'Leave it alone, it's my garden.' Maybe it would be because he never took the time to learn the names of the flowers she planted, or to buy her books about plants and enrol her in a horticultural society with a burgundy enamel badge.

His bladder fills and he searches for a secluded spot. He sometimes is caught short and rushes under trees to relieve himself. Maybe he has done more than this while his trousers are undone, but he is careful to make sure that nobody is looking.

He circuits the playing field, climbing up the other side. There are joggers running together in a group around the playing field now. He is grateful to have missed them. There is a tennis tournament in the town each summer of some prestige. Sometimes he passes joggers with faces he recognises from the sports pages. He has stood in the town, on the back streets, staring up at the specially erected stands, listening to the crowds cheer, to the tannoy announcements and player introductions. Maybe he had a wife who went each year; maybe he wonders why he did not try to share her interests.

At the cliffside now, he does not walk close to the edge. There are warning signs but people do not pay attention to them. They stand with their toes over the edge, peering down. It would be the briefest of moments for the cliff to crack, detach, and they would be gone. Down on the beach couples sit against the cliff, grateful of a place to rest their backs, mindless of the danger they put themselves in. He does not even like to sit below light fittings in theatres; he has, over the years, made note of the seat numbers he has no wish to sit in again. Maybe he once asked his wife to swap seats with him and knew that something had shifted. Previously he had risked the danger rather than place his wife in harm's way.

He passes the point where once he saw a young couple sit while their child ran toward the edge and looked over and they paid him no mind. It left an uneasy feeling in the pit of his stomach and when he turned back a few minutes later the three of them were nowhere to be seen, though he had a full view of everywhere they could have got to in those minutes, he thought. An unhappy young couple, money troubles, or terminal illness, letting their child fall so they too could then follow him. His mind flooded with these thoughts. But, if he was right, it was too late and he walked away from their sad tragedy. At home he scanned the news channels and newspapers, but there was nothing. When he walked the cliffs again he stopped at this spot, tentatively looking over the edge. Below, another grassy outcrop, no more than two feet down, with a winding footpath down to the beach. On a ledge further down were the burnt remains of a tent. Another time he passed three topless teenage boys here, their perfect bodies prompting an ache inside him for when he had not been ashamed to see his own body in the mirror. 'Five years, man,' they shouted on seeing the tent below. 'It's still there, man.'

Here and there, amongst the trees and wild grasses, are discarded troughs. He wonders if animals grazed here once, wonders what stopped them careering off the edge. He thinks this about the dogs he passes untethered from their owners. Maybe if he had once been a drunkard he would have awoken one morning to find himself huddled in one of these troughs, an early morning jogger checking if he was all right, his face a mixture of concern and disgust.

He has reached the point where sometimes he turns back, but not today. This is the biggest slope. It is hard to climb; the tendons in his ankles click in protest. Walking this circuit in reverse there is nothing to do but run down. He has done this many times, feeling elated, the momentum such it is impossible to stop until well after he has reached the bottom. He knows one day he may well fall, may well break a bone. He will be grateful then for the way voices carry up here.

An elderly couple picnic near the top of the slope, their sandwiches and cakes spread across a checked blanket. It does not seem possible for them to have perched themselves on this incline. They both laugh as he passes. 'We can feel the slope pulling us,' they say. 'If you see us rolling down later, do push us back up.' He laughs naturally along with them and this lifts his spirits. He misses his parents then, the moment gone as easily as it came. Maybe he is relieved they did not live to see the outcome of his married life. Maybe, had they lived, it would not have happened. His parents had cast their sway on many of his decisions simply by being a presence in the world.

He climbs the crest of the hill and the ground falls away again below him to the left. Here is a notorious suicide spot, and beyond it the red and white striped lighthouse. Car tracks weave from side to side through the grassy slope, as if the driver had given himself time to change his mind. They disappear over the edge to show he had not. Or she—women killed themselves too. Maybe sometimes he has stood here and wondered what it would be like to fall, if there is calm acceptance of a decision that cannot be reversed, or a stark realisation of a mistaken choice. Maybe, when he used to drink, he stepped several feet back then broke into a breathless run toward the edge, skidding to a halt with inches to spare, just for the fun of seeing people's faces, their reactions, wondering if they would run to stop him. Perhaps after, as he laughed, they wished he had carried on. Maybe he wishes this too.

The lady vicar with her Samaritans sweater prowls the cliff tops. He admires her, curious to know if she has marked him down as one to watch. Does she have time to enjoy the view, or would that feel like a moment she might miss something, the chance to save someone? He casts his eyes around too, noting the old couple still picnicking on the slope behind him, not rolling down yet.

To the right, the road, and a café that has seen better days. He stops here sometimes for a drink, a bite to eat, but today he is not in the mood. The open-top bus has pulled in at the lay-by outside. He has ridden this many times, listening to the history of his town as if he is a stranger here. In some way it does remove him so that when he steps off the bus again into his own town he feels unsure of himself on the streets the bus has travelled down, needing to walk further into the centre of the town, away from the seafront, to feel grounded again.

He turns around now, taking a path that skirts the top of the hills that roll down to the cliff paths he has been walking below. These are paths that disappear between trees. When he meets people coming the other way, particularly if they are in couples or groups, he feels as if he has been caught somewhere he shouldn't be, though these are public footpaths as much as those exposed to view.

Maybe these are the routes he would take if he were out walking with a friend of his daughter.

He walks faster now. The sun is setting. He has been caught out here before when the light has almost gone and the atmosphere changes. Trees and shadows close in, and beneath the canopy of trees he can already barely see. He is grateful when he emerges out again onto the hilltop. Once he took a picture at dusk and, zooming in later on his computer, there was a man staring right at him from behind a distant tree. This has bothered him ever since.

He is back at the slope where he started. He turns and looks back at where he has walked. The cliffs stretch on and on into the distance, some twenty miles can be seen. In his time he has walked all these miles. Maybe if he had a marriage that turned sour, this walking could be what saved him: the endless repetition of one foot in front of the other until blisters form, until the arch of the foot begins to ache, and these pains and aches supplant the ones in his heart and head.

He heads down the slope, resisting the urge to run here, where people can see from the road below. On the main path into town he passes a man who looks older than him, but who may well not be. He is gulping from a can of lager and weaving in and out of his own private, invisible obstacle course. Maybe then he thinks of a married man and the friend of his daughter, heavy with drink, heated with it to such a point that they shed their clothes and frolic in the expensive water feature at the exclusive harbour on the other side of this town. Maybe he thinks of how the handcuffs felt on his bare skin, how the policeman refused to cover his modesty, leaving him standing by the police van as crowds gathered and jeered. Maybe, if he had a daughter, he would not wish her face to be one he spots in the crowd.

He walks fast, this man. Maybe he has somewhere to be. Maybe he has nowhere to be and walking slowly only gives him time to dwell on this.

Maybe he is just a man, out walking.

PUBLICATION CREDITS

Before There Were Houses, This Was All Fields—winner of the Fiction Desk Newcomer Prize 2015 and published in *Long Grey Beard & Glittering Eye* (2015: The Fiction Desk)

A Giant Emerges—longlisted in the National Flash Fiction Day Micro-Fiction Competition (2015)

Little Yellow Squares—winner of the Retreat West Flash Fiction Competition January 2014 and published in *Inside These Tangles, Beauty Lies* (2015: Retreat West)

This Bird She Calls Fear—winner of the Retreat West Short Story Competition June 2014 and published in *Inside These Tangles, Beauty Lies* (2015: Retreat West)

My Fence is Electric—winner of the Paper Swans Flash Fiction competition September 2014 and published in *Paper Swans*, Issue 4 (2014)

Rosa & Thirkel—longlisted (as Rosa, Gathering Sunlight) in the Bristol Short Story Prize (2014) and shortlisted in the Costa Short Story Award (2014). Published online at https://www.costa.co.uk/costa-book-awards/costa-short-story-award/

New House—longlisted in the Bare Fiction Prize for Flash Fiction (2015) and published on the author's website

Tiny Indentations—published in *Firewords Quarterly*, Issue 4 (2015)

Swedish Marbles—longlisted in the RoomtoWrite Short Story Competition (2014)

Sunflower Seeds—winner of the Retreat West Flash Fiction Competition (March 2014) and published in *Inside These Tangles, Beauty Lies* (2015: Retreat West)

Across the Waves—winner of the Paper Swans Flash Fiction competition (May 2014) and published in *Paper Swans*, Issue 4 (2014)

How Easy it is to Break Things Apart—longlisted (as Peckleton & Daughter) in the Homestart Bridgwater Short Story Prize (2015)

Then—highly commended in The Writing Competition (2013) and The New Writer Annual Prose & Poetry Prizes (Micro-Fiction category) (2014) and published on the author's website

Little White Lies—runner-up in the Retreat West Flash Fiction Competition (March 2014) and published in *Inside These Tangles, Beauty Lies* (2015: Retreat West)

Semi-Detached—published online at http://flashfloodjournal.blogspot.com

Smoke Signals—runner-up in the Retreat West Short Story Competition (August 2014) and published in *Inside These Tangles, Beauty Lies* (2015: Retreat West)

White Noise—runner-up in the Retreat West Short Story Competition (May 2014) and published in *Inside These Tangles, Beauty Lies* (2015: Retreat West)

Spreading the Chaos—highly commended in the National Flash Fiction Day Micro-Fiction Competition (2015) and published in *Landmarks: National Flash Fiction Day 2015 Anthology* (2015: Gumbo Press)

A Man, Out Walking—winner of the Vaughan Centre for Life-

long Learning Summer Short Story Competition and published in
the winner's anthology (2015)

ACKNOWLEDGMENTS

Thanks to Amanda Saint for her inspiring monthly competitions at Retreat West and the wonderful authors she asked to judge them—my successes there gave me much needed confidence and spurred me on.

Thanks to all the competitions I entered, whether I was placed in them or not, for getting me to write some words down.

Thanks to *Fiction Desk*, *Firewords Quarterly*, and *Paper Swans* who published my work.

Thanks to Farhana Shaikh for the amazing and supportive work she does for Leicestershire writers. She asks me to stand up in front of people, which I do not like to do, but she always asks so nicely.

Thanks to Rebecca Burns for pointing me toward Odyssey Books.

Thanks to Michelle Lovi and the team at Odyssey Books for believing in me and taking a chance on this collection, and thanks to Michelle for the beautiful cover (I was so worried about the cover—turns out I didn't need to be).

Thanks to my friends Helen, Ian, Deb, and Kim who read these stories first.

Thanks to Mike who has always believed in me and never once doubted he would hold this book in his hands. I love you.

ABOUT THE AUTHOR

Mark Newman has been shortlisted for the Costa Short Story Award, highly commended in the New Writer Prose & Poetry Awards and Bristol Prize longlisted. His work has won competitions judged by Alison Moore, Tania Hershman and David Gaffney. He has been published in *Firewords Quarterly*, *Fiction Desk* and *Paper Swans*. He has eight stories in the Retreat West competition anthology *Inside These Tangles, Beauty Lies*.

Visit Mark at his website:
https://marknewman1973.wordpress.com
or on social media:

facebook.com/myfenceiselectric
twitter.com/FenceIsElectric
instagram.com/myfenceiselectric

www.ingramcontent.com/pod-product-compliance
Lightning Source LLC
Chambersburg PA
CBHW030638190726
48286CB00008B/2576